THE
VANISHING
AT
ECHO LAKE

ALSO BY THE AUTHOR

Renewal
Disconnected
An Unexpected Visit
The Painted Lady
Seeing

JOSEPH FALANK

THE VANISHING AT ECHO LAKE

A NOVEL

Livonia, Michigan

Jacket/Cover Images:
Woods (solarseven)/Shutterstock, Cabin (Joeprachatree)/Shutterstock

THE VANISHING AT ECHO LAKE

Copyright ©2024 Joseph Falank

All rights reserved. No part of this publication may be reproduced, distributed, or transmitted in any form or by any means, including photocopying, recording, or other electronic or mechanical methods, without the prior written permission of the publisher, except in the case of brief quotations embodied in critical reviews and certain other noncommercial uses permitted by copyright law. For permission requests, please write to the publisher.

This book is a work of fiction. The characters, incidents, and dialogue are drawn from the author's imagination and are not to be construed as real. Any resemblance to actual events or persons, living or dead, is entirely coincidental.

Published by BHC Press

Library of Congress Control Number:
20249459534

ISBN: 978-1-64397-409-5 (Hardcover)
ISBN: 978-1-64397-410-1 (Softcover)
ISBN: 978-1-64397-411-8 (Ebook)

For information, write:
BHC Press
885 Penniman #5505
Plymouth, MI 48170

Visit the publisher:
www.bhcpress.com

For my wife, Rebecca—
Who supports every story I am compelled to write,
even the weird ones like this one.

For my kiddos, Maddie and Jack—
Who believe writing a book is the coolest thing in the world.
(It is.)

THE VANISHING AT ECHO LAKE

Echo Lake, NY
About 40 miles east of Serling Oaks
August 30
6:47 a.m.

The mother sparrow broke through the sunlit canopy of leafy whitewoods, towering northern red oaks, white oaks, and various thick and bendy stalks of ash and pine. There were also maples and a few sycamores that filled out the great bed of forest fanning out from the tear-shaped lake. Her view of the water showed a stippling of sunshine fractals on the western edge while the rest of the lake remained in a sleepy shadow slow to recede with the rising daybreak.

She kept low and in proximity to the nest in search of food for her three babies. Their unruly, helpless, and relentless (and yes, perhaps even annoying) pitchy cries for her and their desperation to eat that began promptly at sunup—assaulting her senses in triplicate—spurred within her tiny body like a droning hum that wouldn't be quieted until her offspring had been fed and soothed. A momentous (and repetitive) task, to be sure. Her need to care for and satisfy them drove her every desire and hunter's instinct. While swooping straight down from the nest and being closer to the ground offered the opportunity at a swift bite to snatch up, she found taking a momentary detour above the treetops offered an escape, a moment's respite in the early morning stillness from the demanding triplicate of screeching. Every mother's sought after moment of peace.

But all good things must come to an end.

Cutting back down beneath the crown of the forest, the mother sparrow zeroed in on a number of small insects—some zipping about to and fro in seemingly aimless, weaving trails and some lollying along in lazy straight lines, while others remain stationary as they themselves feed, on the ridged tree trunks—which she readily caught and consumed for herself, then snatched up more to mash up and feed to her nestlings. Upon her hasty return to their little home, forged in the shadow and safety of an inside elbow located up high in the arms of a sprawling white oak, that indisputable maternal siren to appease her babies as quickly as possible turned into a panging alarm of panic. The wide-mouthed hunger cries of the pinkish-gray trio had been reduced in volume by one voice. There were now only two younglings in the nest.

After quickly depositing the buggy puree from her mouth to theirs, the mother sparrow scanned the limbs below, taking flight to search all the way down to the ground in her desperate attempt to locate a fallen, possibly injured baby. Alas, there was not one to find. The mother sparrow's worries turned to seeking out a predator in the skies and surrounding trees, however, that concern was shortly dispelled in her high and low search considering one wasn't found and no enemy would have left the two other vulnerable offspring behind, or at the very least alive. The three would have been killed and taken in short order. Perhaps even the mother sparrow herself as well.

So, what had happened?

Where had her baby gone?

Familiar cries returned, urging the mother sparrow from the floor of the forest back to the nest. When she landed on the branch just outside their bed though, there was but a singular screeching, a vocal longing that was different from the song of their hunger cries. This plea was for protection. One baby remained.

Again, puzzled and frantic, the mother sparrow scanned the other trees above and below for enemies, and again, she found none. She inspected the tree from their perch but neither body of the missing two was anywhere in sight. She examined her lone and whining offspring for wounds but found it completely unscathed, only afraid. There was no reason or source for what had happened. Panic intensified.

Desperate to find what was lost, the mother sparrow cried out her own call for help. Her anguished requiem of chirps, along with her baby's continued whimpering, pierced the calm singsong of the forest, interrupting the morning's otherwise routine serenity with a haunting tune of melancholy.

Echo Lake, NY
August 31
8:15 a.m.

Breakfast may have been the most important meal of the day, but sometimes it was also the biggest chore to clean up after. A bowl of cereal? A package of mini muffins? Some Pop-Tarts? Easy-peasy cleanup there. Clumps of cold scrambled eggs leftover on plates, dried yolk residue caked along the inside of a frying pan, a fair dusting of toast crumbs spread across the tabletop, chair seats, and floor? Pain-in-the-ass cleanup. Didn't help having this task ahead either when fighting a migraine as Marybel had since getting up at quarter after five. An early riser throughout the rest of the year—essential when school was in session so she could have both kids ready for school and herself not looking like a complete disaster before teaching global studies to classes of eighth graders all day—she had continued waking to her alarm over summer break to have that essential "me time." That quiet hour and a half (if she was lucky) while the kids were still immobile in their beds to have her two cups of coffee out on their two-story deck and look out over the water and listen to the birds. To have time for her thoughts, her daydreams. To breathe in that clean lake air scented with wood, leaves, the crisp water, and the dew off the grass. To keep that invaluable hope that summer brings and enjoy the time she had left before having to put on her Mary Janes, her nice slacks, and blouses again instead of her thin sandals (when she wasn't going around barefoot almost all of the time), ultracasual tank tops, and sun-skirts and return to her classroom to begin preparations for the next group of mouthy, hormonal early teens.

Ugh, she thought. *I hope we're not all coming down with something.*

Gabe had woken up saying the front of his head hurt, too. Six-year-olds didn't tend to complain, especially when enjoying the freedom of summer, and Marybel hadn't thought too much of it initially, but now looking at the boy's abandoned plate, it didn't seem he'd had much of an appetite. That, according to any doctor, was usually a sign of concern. Though, Marybel considered, he was also nagging to get outside already and refill the kiddie pool, because again, that was just the nature of six-year-old boys: why not go swimming on a summer day just after eight in the morning? Marybel had shut him down on taking a dip in the lake so early but relented on him unraveling the garden hose and adding a few inches to the wading pool so he could splash around at his own desire.

Come to think of it, Marybel could still hear the low thrum of water running through the basement pipes that led out to the spigot.

"Anna! Can you see if Gabe's finished filling his pool yet?"

Damn. Just calling out from the dining room worsened the ache that kept tightening like a leather belt looped across her eyes around to the back of her skull. Marybel caught an aching throb from the volume of her words as they rang through the fillings in her molars. She let out a gritting hiss while chomping down on the side of her lip, but that did nothing to distract from the pain or ease the tension. She had taken her migraine pill with her orange juice, but that had been about ten minutes ago as they were finishing up breakfast. It would be a little while before it started kicking in.

"Anna! Gabe!"

Where were her kids? Why weren't they answering?

"Anna!"

A door opened—the downstairs bathroom door it sounded like—just off the dining room.

"Hey, everything all right?"

Tatum, a neighbor who lived two houses down on the drive of Bass Lane that circled the lake, came back into the dining room, standing beside Marybel at the table.

"Just a headache." Marybel closed her eyes and pressed with both hands on the pressure points across her brow, hoping to find some relief. "It'll go away."

"Want me to stick around? I can watch the kiddos for a bit, Mare, if you want to go lie down."

Tate's offer was tempting, but Marybel had enough on her plate, literally. Enough to clean off all the plates in front of her, for starters, plus the fact Tate was always offering to stay with Anna and Gabe to give Marybel some free time to go out on her own for a few hours and recharge the batteries. Now that the divorce was final and Henry had proven himself a deadbeat dad by taking off to Phoenix with the new girlfriend, Marybel was doing the duty of two parents, which, in the beginning, wore her out quick. She was used to it now. And though sleeping off her emerging migraine was probably the smarter option, Marybel was ready to stop relying on her friend's goodwill to get by. She was determined to grin and bear it.

"No, it's okay. Thanks, Tate."

"Sure. No problem." Tate gave a supportive rub on Marybel's back. "Call if you need anything. I'll be home all day. Lou and I are just going to be out in the yard. We're still cleaning up from that storm on Sunday."

"That was quite the storm that came through. I saw where some trees around here had come down. Hey, if you see my children on your way home, can you tell them to come inside?"

"Absolutely, dear."

"Thank you."

Marybel kept her head down in her massaging hands, listening for Tate, whose foam flip-flops were smacking at the bottoms of her feet, to finish going down the deck steps to the yard before forcing herself up. Dragging her own bare and thickly calloused feet to the kitchen, Marybel took the forehead thermometer out of the medicine cabinet, pointed it at the spot just above the bridge of her nose (thinking how strange it was that so many of these types of thermometers had a gun shape to them), and pulled the trigger. Two seconds and one confirmation *beep* later, the readout screen glowed green, revealing her temperature.

97.7

Normal.

"Huh."

She did it again.

Normal. Only a tenth of a degree less this time.

She took it a third and fourth time, to be sure. It had been long reported and documented how inaccurate such external thermometers really were, but, experience-wise, Marybel found them to be much closer to true than not. Both additional times she was given normal results.

"Must just be a migraine then."

That offered some relief anyway as she returned the temporal thermometer to the cabinet. That low thrum of running water pushing through the maze of basement copper pipes was the only disruption in the otherwise quiet home.

"Anna! Gabe!"

That hurt. A deep, dull squeeze of pressure from the top of her head to the muscles beneath her jaw. And all wasted effort if her kids were outside where they couldn't hear her. Marybel grimaced as she went to the door and stepped outside. The brightened world, warming up with an underscore of rising humidity that had produced a thin fog on the lake bed, did her eyes and her head no favors. She didn't feel confident taking the long staircase down to the grass to perform a search around the house and instead remained clutching the wood railing of the deck while, once more, calling out for her children. Again, neither gave an answer.

It wasn't like them to ignore her calls, to wander off, or to go play somewhere else…

They also wouldn't leave the outside water running…

"Gabe! Anna!"

Shouting for her kids hurt her head like hell, but the pain was no longer a concern.

Worry for the unknown whereabouts of her kids permeated through every open pore, worming into her unsettled, cramping stomach. Marybel stood at the top of the stairs nauseous with a creeping, escalating panic.

As she pressed fingers deep into the sides of her brow, her instincts rang alarms in tandem with every cry of their names. She couldn't sense them anywhere nearby…

"Anna! Gabe!"

Where the hell did they go?

Southside Serling Oaks, NY
September 4
1:42 p.m.

Ben and Kelsey Renmore kissed their three kids goodbye. The trio of youngsters—Margaret (5) and twins Ryan and Ben Jr. (3)—fresh from playing in the backyard with their ragged breaths, sweaty brows, breeze-tossed hair, grass-stained shins and knees, and sunbeat faces, waved from the sunken red-brick walk in front of their modest ranch-style home as the couple packed their backpacks and a cooler into the trunk space of their Toyota 4Runner.

"And what did we discuss earlier?" Ben asked as a reminder after closing the liftgate.

The children chorused, *"Not to talk about tooting!"*

Ben shot them a thumbs-up before trotting over and mussing up the boys' sweat-slicked hair. With his thumb and forefinger he applied a stroke to his daughter's bony jaw ending with a gentle pinch of her chin. "Love you guys." He gave each of his children a last kiss on the delicate and damp centers of their foreheads, feeling the heat exuding from their flushed skin, before stepping back on the uneven front walk where blades of unruly grass and weeds reached up through the cracks and splits between the bricks.

"Love you," said Margaret in return.

"Wuv you," echoed the twins with a giggle.

"Listen to grandma," said Kelsey after climbing into the passenger seat. She swept her shoulder-length blond hair up into a clip to get it off her sweating neck now that she was stationary in the warm car. "Do everything she says." Grandma—Ben's mother, Sheila—stood on the threshold, holding the front screen door wide open, waving and offering her reassurances ("Everything will be just fine," "We're gonna have so much fun," and for them to "Have a good trip"). Meanwhile, two girthy and noisy flies that were cutting circles around the front porch zipped past her unaware and into the house, niggling at Ben's impatience.

"All right, kiddos…" Eager to get things in motion (and not allow more insects to have unrequited access to their home) with midafternoon setting in, Ben hopped in, adjusted the driver's seat from his wife's fixed position to accommodate his long legs, and started up the engine. He and Kelsey had about an hour's drive ahead of them—longer maybe depending on local traffic getting to the highway—that he (and pretty sure she) wasn't looking forward to.

Kelsey called out one last time before they were in motion, backing down the steep grade of their driveway onto Charleston Lane. "We'll miss you guys! Love you!"

Only Margaret answered back with a "Byeeeeee!" as the children dashed away from the walk and raced past their grandmother inside the house, the front door closing tight behind them.

And just like that, unceremoniously, it was over.

Kelsey let out all of the air held in her lungs in a despondent huff. "How quickly we become chopped liver."

"We're always chopped liver when Grandma's here. They know she'll give them anything they want."

Pulling away, Ben noticed Kelsey's gaze follow the house passing by out her window—a window that featured unwashed fingerprint smudges from Margaret on both sides of the pane—with longing as it fell into their rearview.

She asked, "How much you want to bet they're already begging her for ice cream?"

"Ice cream?" Ben sputtered a cynical raspberry. "Right now they're definitely digging into that huge tray of chocolate chip cookies she brought with her. Ice cream will be what's for dinner."

Kelsey replied, "Oy…" And in that loathing in her voice Ben had recently become all too familiar with, he heard his wife's eyes rolling all the way around in her head. He felt that very same distaste knowing their children would be spoiled rotten with an abundance of sweets during their night away. But, he reconciled, that was a problem for later.

"Time to get this show on the road." Ben made the left turn off Charleston. The quiet hum of the 4Runner's engine, the gentle wind carrying the churn of lawn mowers and trimmers and the fragrance of cut grass came through the cracked open windows, along with the subtle chattering of cicadas, all conjoined into a soundtrack of nature and serenity that did nothing to help them relax.

Their neighborhood long out of view, heading for the highway via the on-ramp half a mile down the road, Ben and Kelsey each took a deep inhale that was weighted in their own apprehensions and let it out slowly.

"They'll be fine," Ben said, the assuredness in his voice meant to convince himself as well. "They'll be spoiled and have blood sugar levels that would send a diabetic into a coma, but they'll be fine."

After a brief interlude of indecisiveness, he laid a hand atop of his wife's on the padded column between their seats in an effort to be reaffirming only to draw it away when she remained limp and unresponsive. It was a form of rejection he'd become all too familiar with. He cursed himself for even trying, and evasion became the name of the game. Ben slinked his shunned hand back to the steering wheel so he could swap grips and press the down switch for his window at the control panel on the driver's side door. The roar of passing wind filling the cabin as they traveled seventy on Highway 17 East out of town, pursuant to Ben's method of avoidance, was also vanquished when Kelsey (passive-aggressively) reached forward on the dashboard console and dialed on the air-conditioning.

Up then went the windows, leaving them to occupy a muted vehicle, save for the muffled sounds of passersby and the soft current of chilled air whispering out of the many dashboard vents.

Now they either had to talk or resume sitting in uncomfortable silence for the duration of the drive. Switching on the radio felt like a deliberate and sophomoric act to dodge conversation with his wife. But, given the current state of their union, Ben wasn't above such behaviors. He dabbed the button for the radio, and the speakers started blasting kiddie tunes by the Laurie Berkner Band from one of the programmed stations set for the kids. Ben was keen to let it ride, even quietly singing along to "I'm Gonna Catch You" before Kelsey made another selection, jumping over to one of her saved country favorites. She dropped the volume so their voices wouldn't be drowned out. Ben's insides cramped up with expectation.

"It's just a temporary separation, Kelsey. It's not permanent."

The conversation was inevitable. Unavoidable. Ben considered that it was better to get it out and over with before they were forced to put on an act for the friends they were meeting up with for the long weekend. This was their first time speaking of the mutual agreement made the evening before, following another of their endless go-arounds after the kids were asleep. Ben couldn't remember what exactly had started their most recent fight, but anymore it didn't take much kindling to ignite a brush fire. Such as it was, he didn't want to downplay the gravity of their decision, one that would shake the very foundation of their once sturdy family of five. He made sure to be sincere when he added, "At least I hope it's not permanent."

He glanced her way for any kind of response when she didn't say anything, didn't pledge any kind of intention—didn't retract from or further commit to the plans they'd (hastily) established in the heat of last night's moment. Just continued staring out the passenger side glass. The only outward sign of her discomfort with the conversation, though this didn't speak to whether or not she would participate, was seen in how she kept fixing the hem of her blue-and-orange sundress over her short, shapely legs that she kept crossing and uncrossing at the ankles. Ben wasn't going to force the issue and create a whole new situation. Wasn't worth it. He couldn't make his wife talk, and so he resigned himself to the radio and the engine taking over the soundtrack of their trip while the miles continued adding up.

"It's just…"

Ben encouraged her. "Just what?"

"Just…" Kelsey shook her head. "Just doesn't feel right to be parading around acting like we haven't been having problems for months. No one knows anything, and we have to pretend to be…different."

"You think we should tell our friends? Kind of an odd thing to share out of the blue when we haven't gotten together like this in almost two years, don't you think? 'Hey, guys, how's it going? Good? Yeah, the kids are great—probably all sugar high and throwing up gallons of ice cream and chunks of cookies, but they're good. Oh, us? Yeah, we're just gonna take a break from each other for a bit. No biggie.'" He wasn't trying to be facetious, and apologized if that's how he sounded, but he also needed Kelsey to know their world couldn't be all doom and gloom—hadn't COVID and twenty-four-hour cable news done enough of that already? Plus, they hadn't yet acted on their decision. "Things can still change in the next few days. It's all up to us."

Kelsey let the words and their significance have their time before she sighed, sounding a little more at ease and convinced. "You're right."

"I'm sorry?"

She smirked at him. "Yeah, I know. Don't get used to it."

Ben exhaled a small laugh, feeling a bit more at ease. A little more loosened up. He didn't quite realize how tense he had become. His lanky body caught a head-to-toe chill from the blowing air-conditioning that was cooling the breakout sweat that had emitted from how rigid he was sitting. He also, strangely, felt a little empowered in the moment, a little proud that he'd contributed something of value to their situation and, by way of that, their marriage. Which made him talk more.

"Last night you said you didn't even want to go on this trip anymore. Think about it: if we didn't go, everyone would know something's up. But no one has to know what's going on with us, Kelsey. It's not like it's obvious or that we're living a lie. It's not written on our foreheads like the scarlet letter. We're still wearing our rings. We're just not sharing any news. Maybe we will, maybe we won't. We don't owe that to anyone. We don't need to go announcing everything to the world and changing our status on Facebook. We only decided on this last night. Maybe it will stay the same, or maybe it will change. We can only do what's best for us right now. What's best for us and best for the kiddos. Best for us all in the long term anyway.

"We've had this plan for the lake house with everyone for months. And honestly…after all the crazy shit we've been through…we need it. We need to get past this whole pandemic thing and see our friends. We need to catch up. We need to be around other adults. We need to hear what's going on with others and have conversations and have other things on our minds. One of our biggest problems, even before the pandemic kept us all at home, has been that we don't make the time to do things together. If we cancel on everyone now, we'll just be home and miserable and start to argue, and please say something or else I'm just going to keep talking."

Desperate, he looked her way, exasperated and resembling the grimacing emoji face, realizing he was rambling the same points they'd been over ad nauseam. He hoped the anguished chuckle he emitted would nab him—and them as a struggling couple—just a little more ground along the path of reprieve.

Kelsey blinked, unmoved, and quipped, "You know…I already said you were right."

Ben cut a smiling grimace as he nervously scratched at the buzzed, graying side of his head and tousled the medium length of brown hair on top he kept purposefully messy. He hoped he hadn't just put a reverse on their progress. "Should have just taken my victory and left it alone, huh?"

She was snappy in her reply, but there was a smile to be found in Kelsey's blue eyes. "Yup."

Ben nodded, satisfied, and focused his eyes fully back on the long stretch of road that was 17 taking them east, content to let the subject rest. The scenic vistas through rural upstate were characterized by the many patches of dense woods and short hillsides of wild grass and a plethora of dandelion and henbit and white clover. There were also farmlands, some derelict barns, and crop fields at the height of their offerings, some beginning to brown and wane. Peaceful scenery above all else. For Ben, he could now enjoy the view by way of the tranquility that came from establishing peace in the car. Perhaps it was a temporary peace, but it was still a peace that was achieved and new enough to allow a moment to breathe. "Look at us agreeing on things."

Kelsey added, "Doesn't happen often."

Her hand remained on the column rest between them. This time, when he placed his hand on hers, she accepted his touch and offered him a short but tight squeeze in return. It wasn't lasting, but like their current status of amity, it was enough.

With about forty minutes left in their drive, Kelsey turned up the volume on the radio. Ben didn't take exception. Probably better that they didn't speak the entire time, especially now that they'd reached a consensus, a good and stable coexistence. Opportunities to talk afforded him more opportunities to say the wrong things. That he had a great tendency for as well. Kelsey rolled the dial in search of something free of static, settling on a famous artist's twangy tune she knew the lyrics to and sang along. Classic country wasn't his station of choice, but for the sake of their newfound wellbeing, Ben was determined to let that slide and even sing along.

New York State Route 17-E
10 miles from Echo Lake
2:24 p.m.

When her husband cut a hard swerve on the linear stretch of highway, Denna Meers's eyes popped open, and a breath snagged in her throat. Though the seat belt held her during the sudden but violent jostle, her reflexes were that of an unamused cat trying to avoid a bathtub as she cast out both hands and feet in every direction—latching on to the grip of the door and pressing against the sidewalls of the floor well and clutching the center armrest to keep from being thrown around.

"What the heck was that about?"

"Garbage bag in the middle of the road," Teddy answered, peering curiously into the Wrangler's rearview, not phased at all by his sudden jerky maneuvering.

Denna cut a quick look back over her headrest. "A garbage bag? You nearly slammed me against the door to avoid a garbage bag?"

In the growing distance she caught a glimpse of a mostly flat, fluttering, white ghost of a form sitting next to the road's dotted line. The bag billowed and flattened, changing its size and shape with the summery wind coming across the verdant fields. Its tapered crown kicked up in the slipstream created by their passing. Whatever was discarded inside kept it weighed down on the pavement.

Teddy was quick on the defensive. "There could be a body in it."

Denna rolled her eyes, dismissive of her husband's neurosis. "There wasn't a body in the bag."

"Correction," Teddy said, emphasizing with a pointer finger aimed at the sky. "There is never a zero percent chance of there being no body in a bag."

He surveyed the rearview again for his own peace of mind. The world being what it was after such a dark shift in 2016, no human act, no matter how despicable, could be overlooked. A whole faction of people today was seemingly fine with caging immigrant children. If these people could hold such a heartless stance publicly, Teddy worried what dark possibilities lurked within the worst of us and what they were capable of when no one was looking. He'd seen enough episodes of *Dateline* to know better. "What if some deranged mother put her baby in a garbage bag and left it on the side of the road?"

Denna cringed at the posed hypothetical. "That's absolutely horrible." She then gave his arm a smack. "And why does it have to be a mother? There are some equally terrible, if not *worse*, fathers out there."

"That reminds me," said Teddy. "You know that'll be the first thing everyone is going to ask us about."

Denna scrunched her freckle-spattered nose while taking her phone off the magnetic mount that was affixed high on the dash. "What are you talking about?"

"You being pregnant."

Denna's head slightly tilted. "Except the thing is I'm not pregnant."

"Exactly!"

"You're nuts." She swept the right side of her chin-length auburn hair behind her ear and reviewed the directions on the Maps app. Checking the group chat she'd set up in Messenger for everyone meeting at the lake house, Denna saw the last entry in the communication thread was her own, saying to the others *See you all there!*, that she'd sent out late last night. She wished to sidestep the conversation her husband was initiating, not granting any further acknowledgment. "This says we should be getting to Woodstock in about seven miles."

Teddy ignored the announcement of how close they were to their destination. He was operating on a one-track mind, feeling his agenda was imperative to discuss so they could be on the same page.

"We haven't done the group thing with these guys in almost two years, Dee—of course they're going to ask, especially when they see you're still thin as a rail."

"Thanks? Was that a compliment? You're so sweet." Scrolling through Facebook for as long as there was still a decent 5G signal, Denna maintained eyes on her phone. It wouldn't be much longer before they arrived at the small lakeside abode at Echo Lake that was their destination for the night. Residing just outside the town of Woodstock, the lake house was owned and offered to her by John, a work friend, and came with all the amenities—full working kitchen, grill, a woodstove (if needed on a chilly night), a dock and paddleboat, and the perennial great outdoors exclusive: spotty cell reception. "Besides, nobody cares that I'm not pregnant, Teddy."

"Have you met our friends? They're *parents*, Dee. Parents are always wondering why other married couples without kids *don't* have kids. It's like some kind of parenthood cult."

When it couldn't be ignored, the best way Denna had found to disengage from a conversation she didn't want to have with her husband was to keep throwing out different subjects. Akin to fishing, the more lines she cast the better hope she'd eventually snag a catch and Teddy's mind would latch on to some other train of thought. There was also the option of napping for the rest of the ride, or at least pretending to sleep, but her husband had already demonstrated a knack for quickly swerving to avoid mysterious bags in the middle of the road.

"Hear anything new from Bryan?" she asked. "Is he ever planning to expand your store's hours and make you a full-time, forty-hours-per-week employee again? Target's employees aren't having *their* hours cut."

Asking Teddy about work was sure to exasperate him, but the tactic did the trick and got his mind elsewhere.

"Dee, Target isn't having the same revenue problems as us because people need milk and eggs and tampons. The *essentials*. We sell Blu-rays and lightning cables and e-readers. They aren't essential."

"I bet Bryan's working forty hours a week though," quipped Denna.

"He's the regional manager. He's got like a dozen stores to manage. He doesn't have time to talk to me."

"A dozen stores that are only open from eleven to six."

Teddy argued, "But they're still open."

"Yeah, well, funny you say that because it looks like one just closed."

Denna thumbed through a post on her Facebook feed and its comments. "Matter-of-fact, it's the fourth one in the state."

"What? Where are you reading that?"

She held up her phone, turning the screen to him. She summed up the subject line, so his attention didn't linger too long off the road. "The one in the Syracuse mall."

The enormity of this news brought his shoulders, which had been tense, to sink. His response to the story was a drawn-out groan.

Denna remarked, "Looks like Regional Manager Bryan just got a little bit of extra time to talk to you."

Teddy had every reason to fret. The TechWorld store at Syracuse's Destiny USA—one of the largest indoor shopping centers on the East Coast—had been in a prime spot as one of the mall's anchor tenants. However, the company as a whole never fully recovered following the months-long closures that had come with the initial stay-at-home orders declared in the Northeast at the onset of the COVID-19 spread. To save money when reopening, TechWorld had shortened their business hours and shifted their focus to being a "curbside, pickup-order" retailer. A skeleton crew was kept on hand to fulfill orders and mitigate financial losses. The longer the pandemic choked the life out of the economy, the more tough decisions had to be made to compensate and balance the scales. TechWorld had pivoted much of its business model to its retail website because, simply, it was another instance of being cost-effective and required less capital to run. Consumers weren't spending because incomes were tight, and a lack of wages affected spending for those whose work had been permanently shuttered. Careful decisions on expenses had to be made, buying strictly what was needed, like groceries and gas, and paying to keep the lights on instead of shelling out for iTunes gift cards.

As the store manager at the Serling Oaks location, Teddy worked throughout, but only at a weekly maximum of thirty hours—receiving what shipments came in, devising schedules to give his employees as many hours as he was allowed, reconfiguring the store layout to meet the slight uptick in pickup orders—but the writing was on the wall. It was all just a matter of time.

And what then?

"It might be time to start looking," Denna suggested, and not for the first time. Treading over previously covered ground initiated a dizzying spell of déjà vu. Trying to convince her husband to look elsewhere for employment opportunities, wanting him to dream of something bigger for himself, for them, for the potential growth of their family (which he was set on), had been one of the few failures she'd endured throughout her marriage.

"Look where?" Teddy asked, knowing very well that options were limited for a retail supervisor in the current landscape.

"Anywhere," Denna quietly replied. She returned her phone onto the fixed mount then slumped back against the seat with her arms crossed, not finding the will to engage in another round on this topic.

Coming up ahead on the right shoulder was a broken-down, navy blue pickup. Scratches, cancerous rust, and pockmarks that could have been the result of a shower of hailstones riddled the body. The tailgate was down with the bed crusted with dirt. The bumper was all dinged up and featured a sticker of the Confederate flag which hung askew and sun-faded. Both tires on the driver's side were flat, one wheel missing its hubcap. A tan plastic grocery bag was pinched in the rolled-up window, left to fly as a crude wind sock.

Teddy sneered with revulsion as they passed by. "There is definitely a body in there."

Echo Lake, NY
2:32 p.m.

John didn't like to be a focal point of attention. He didn't like to answer questions as if he were some Realtor, didn't like playing host and welcoming guests, and he certainly wasn't feeling up to being a tour guide for the property or its surrounding lake community, so the hope was to be long gone by the time Denna and her friends arrived.

Opening the passenger side door of his three-decade-old red Dodge Ram panel van, he was greeted with a squawk of grinding metal that flared gooseflesh up the back of his neck. He tossed onto the clothed passenger seat two large kitchen bags stuffed with a couple weeks' worth of trash. By himself he didn't accumulate a whole lot of trash. Down in the footwell he stuck a blue recycle bin filled to the top with empty cans of Black & Tan and hollowed-out bottles of various IPAs. He did, on the other hand, consume a fair bit of alcohol by himself. Having spent the last week at the lake, secluded in his favorite vacation spot, he had a plan to stop at the dump on his way back to town, but he couldn't leave just yet. A check of his watch indicated he was cutting it close—very close considering he wanted to mow the grass before heading out—and thus grumbled his personal favorite curse.

"Bitch nuggets."

Denna had told him she expected to arrive close to three, with the others in tow or not far behind. To believe he could cut the mangy, shin-high grass, which covered about a quarter of an acre between the front yard wrapping around one side of the ranch-style house and leading down a shallow hill out back to a dirt-and-stone path extending from the dock area, in less than half an hour wasn't an entirely unreasonable charge. John's motivation was his aversion to people. It's why he spent most of his free time up at the lake—had been there the past week before schools opened and before what he called "lake opportunities" dwindled. Between the choice of city noises, city smells, and city congestion (chalk it all up as *city problems*) against the relaxing isolation, the privacy, and the serene surroundings, well, it really wasn't a choice at all.

Where most of his eleven other neighbors on Bass Lane only used their places as a summer residence, John was looking forward to—and working toward—the day when his little spot on Echo Lake would become a forever getaway. Having a woodstove installed a few years prior had freed him from having to button the place up come winter. In fact, the off-season months were some of his favorite times to visit on a weekend or school-afforded break. Autumntime revealed the richest colors and most beautiful imagery to go along with the constant fragrance of burning wood. Winter offered a frozen blanket of quiet calm over the lake and its surrounding woodlands unlike anything else. Once he was ready to retire and add a few more amenities—a large TV with good internet service to stream, for one, because cable was too expensive for what was now a temporary sanctum and even for later was still unnecessary—John could say he would be living in his all-time dream home.

Put in one more school year, anyway. Maybe.

The physical wear of his job had long taken its toll. At sixty-six, John Carey had given almost thirty-five years to the Catholic school system as a head custodian. Coming away from his career, he would have bad knees, a sore back, and while he wasn't swimming in riches à la Scrooge McDuck, he would have a small pension to help carry him through. No longer would he have to rely on renting out the lake house to put a few extra bucks in his wallet. Not having to pay $800 a month for his apartment back in Oaks would also help stabilize his finances in his retired years.

The thought of rentals spurred him back to the next task at hand.

They'll all be here soon. And you don't want to be.

John hopped in the van that was parked askew on the lawn out front. The engine took a bit of coaxing to turn over since it hadn't been started in over a week, groaning and cranking due to its age, but it did cough itself to life. John backed the vehicle down around the side of the house, stepped out, and felt a little wobbly on his knees. He winced at a throb that had been strengthening all morning just above his eyes. His mouth had gone as dry as the Sahara. The hasty exit from the driver's seat put his head in a hazy spin that instigated the arrival of little spots here and there across his vision.

Gotta stop the day drinking.

The day drinking was also responsible for the potbelly he carried around, but to be fair, when John was at the lake, he operated on "lake time," which was his reasoning (a better word for *excuse*) to do what he wanted when he wanted and not conform to other socially acceptable standards. At sixty-six though, he knew full well (just buried deep in a mental well) that those choices were no longer consequence free.

Get through the work now, and later you can toss on a movie in the apartment and take a nice long siesta in the recliner.

John considered how good of an idea that was and grunted approval. Funny how, later in life, such bargains had become strong motivators. After blinking away the dissipating spots and taking a deep breath to help reorient himself and regain his wits, he pulled open the back panel doors of the van. Stashed inside, beside the few red gasoline containers of various volumes, was a push mower amongst other yard work equipment that was all individually labeled *Property of the Catholic Schools of Serling Oaks*. Not that any of his bosses would mind, John believed. Likely, they didn't even know he borrowed it on many occasions.

Bringing the mower down to the grass caused his back to bark at him a little.

Twenty minutes. You can do this.

Again, he grunted an approval to inspire himself.

It took a few drags on the starter rope after priming the engine to get the mower chewing away, but like his van, the engine got going. John had just settled into the cadence of his walk behind the self-propelled mower, creating a buzzed path a few yards in, when the blades got snagged, the output chute clogged, and the engine stalled.

"Great." John scraped his teeth over the pasty surface of his tongue and spat out the foamy, cottony residue. The grass had gotten too tall. He'd need to raise the deck on the mower or else it would just keep quitting on him. Except when he knelt to adjust the deck level, he got dizzy again. His head started pounding to the point that there were dull, echoey palpitations in his ears.

Too dehydrated...

John used the mower handle to help him stand back up, his knees giving an unsteady wobble. The back of his shirt was now stuck to him, drenched from sweat, and tears welled from the pain in his head. He thought there might still be some ibuprofen inside to take for the headache (and the other pains gnawing at him). Definitely, he needed water.

About halfway to the house, he realized he had locked both front doors and the keys were in the van.

Bitch nuggets.

The exertion of returning to the van and reaching up over the wheel to pull the key ring out of the ignition was more taxing than it should have been. John recognized there wasn't much he could do about how he felt just yet and grunted his way up into the driver's seat so he could easily remove the keys, ending the relentless and oh-so-annoying chime of the key-in-ignition alert. That feat having been done, he leaned himself back into the seat, lolling his pulsing head against the rest and uttered a throaty sigh.

He could sleep if he wanted to. And he wanted to.

The keys slipped from his loose grasp, falling to the carpeted floor between the seats.

They'll be here soon. Gotta get up.

John was barely able to grunt an affirmative.

Gotta finish...

He decided he would give himself one minute. One minute and he would count down in his head. Then he would muster what he needed to, drag himself out of the van, go in the house for water and ibuprofen, and finish cutting the damn grass. Then he'd be on his way.

John muttered.

He closed his eyes and started to count.

Woodstock, NY
2:47 p.m.

A mile farther along 17-E, a blue sign with yellow printing on the roadside welcomed them to the town of Woodstock, which appeared abruptly out of the broad surroundings of lush fields with swaying asters and willows and ash trees. Their leaves were only just hinting at their autumnal colors but weren't shy of mold spots. Short of the charming block-wide community square of modern businesses occupying restored historic buildings set around a freshly paved one-way oval was a Mirabito gas station. Teddy signaled to pull in.

"We're getting gas now?" Denna asked.

He parked at pump number two and pulled a lever under the dash to pop the gas cover.

"So we don't have to stop tomorrow. Want anything inside?"

Denna squinted and shifted her puckered lips side to side, considering. "You should see if they're hiring."

"Funny." Teddy frowned at his wife, opened the door, and stepped out. The early September air was warm with the remembrance of summer winding down and slightly muggy for the middle of the afternoon with the sun past its apex, but the easy wind that passed through the town square off the fields and rich hillsides brought an edge, a promise to be kept of the coming and eventual autumn. The crisp scent of sun-warmed dirt and wilting grass and crops across the fields, along with the oily pungence of gasoline, filled Teddy's nose as he took a mind-cleansing breath. In long white basketball shorts featuring the famous designer swoosh and brown leather sandals, he didn't feel a chill on his legs or feet (both coated in erratic waves of thick hair that rivaled the mythical yeti), but his forearms did produce a rash of goose bumps that brought him to roll down the sleeves of his hoodie.

After swiping his Mastercard, Teddy inserted the nozzle and closed his eyes, listening solely to the steady gush of fuel entering the tank, thankful not to hear his wife continue talking about how he needed to find a new job. The tank in the Jeep Wrangler was only depleted to half, so they didn't actually need to refill yet. They could have made the return trip home the next day, and the needle would have maybe dropped to the next notch down the gauge, but the change in the vehicle's interior atmosphere, brought on by Denna's will to be heard, necessitated the time-out of pulling into the station. Teddy had only just started to breathe freely, enjoying the fragrant bouquet of unleaded gasoline, when a familiar voice broke his concentration on the nothingness of the moment.

"Guess they'll let anyone get gas here."

Next to Teddy at the pump was his friend Ben filling up his 4Runner.

"Only losers," added Teddy. "Guess that explains why you're here, too."

Ben chuckled while removing the nozzle from the intake and set it back in the holster on the pump. "How are you, man?"

The pump made a *clunk*, and Teddy finished filling the tank with light squeezes, rounding up to the next dollar. "Good. Good. How about you guys?" Teddy shot a lift of his chin at Kelsey when he saw her through the driver's side window. The two friends recapped their respective fuel lids.

"Doing great also," said Ben. He folded his arms and leaned back against the driver's side door. "Can't believe it's been so long. How'd you guys do with COVID?"

Teddy shook his head. "Never got it. Either of us. How bout you guys?"

"I actually got hit with it back in…November? Yeah, early November last year. Our whole house was quarantined right up to Thanksgiving. Wasn't too bad. Had a fever for a couple of nights. Couple of times I got up at like two in the morning drenched in sweat. No cough though. Maybe a little achiness. Chills a little bit, but nothing terrible. Kelsey and the kids didn't get it—thank God."

"Ah, yeah," Teddy agreed. "That's great—I mean that no one else in your house got it and it wasn't worse for you. You're good though? I heard some people were long-haulers or something, still dealing with it months later or had, like, organ damage or erectile dysfunction."

"Oh yeah, no, that wasn't me. Totally fine now. Everything still works.

To tell you the truth, I think the side effects from the vaccine hit me harder. Definitely, the second shot nailed me down for a good twenty-four hours."

"Oh, so you guys got vaccinated."

"Yeah. Yeah, we did. Especially with Kelsey teaching and being around kids all day and my mom being around our kids. Couldn't take the chance and risk it, you know? Did you guys get the shot?"

"Uh, no…no, we didn't."

"Oh." Ben scratched his stubbly chin for an exorbitant amount of time. "So, you guys still do the mask thing? Have you thought about getting one of the vaccines?"

"Uh, no…" An expression of guilt and surprise in his uneasy, toothy smile, Teddy periscoped around to see if anyone else walking across the lot was privy to their conversation. "No, we're just…pretty much…you know…playin' it as it lies." He said this last part while pantomiming a golf putt, adding in a clucking of his tongue off the roof of his mouth to insinuate connecting with the ball.

A subtle split second of disappointment sobered Ben's demeanor—mostly in his dropping gaze and the tight squeeze he afforded his lips—that he attempted to hide by putting a fist to his mouth and clearing his throat. Teddy anticipated this reaction and felt a knock of shame when actually exposed to it. He and Denna knew their outlook on the pandemic (dangerous to those with weaker immune systems and mildly bothersome to those who were stronger and upped their vitamin intake) and their choice in how they protected themselves would not be popular or preferable or even accepted and understood by their friends. Especially Ben, who'd begun acting cautious about the virus back when they were all last together in December 2019 for the birth of their friend Pete's daughter. Back when COVID had yet to enter the United States but was coming with the promise of being "significantly disruptive" to everyday life. Teddy just hoped none of his and Denna's choices in how they managed themselves over the last two years would have come up, silly as that hope was. But now it was out there—front-page news—and they hadn't even all gathered at the lake house yet. A sign of things to come, perhaps. A harbinger of doom. The elephant in the room had farted, letting everyone know it was there.

Ben recovered quickly, sounding off with a random changeup. "Speaking of things still working… Are you guys—" He popped up on tiptoes, eyebrows raised, peering across the pumps at Denna slouched in the passenger seat, bare feet up on the dash, phone in hand, thumbs performing a tap dance on the screen. "You guys pregnant yet?"

Teddy wielded the same expression of dissatisfaction and uneasy guilt to account for this delinquency. An expectation from their friends he'd seen coming miles away. "Uh, no…no, not yet. Maybe soon though? Never know…"

"Oh. Well." Ben itched his chin again. "Anything else we can talk about that'll make this even more awkward?"

Both guys chuckled, uncomfortable at first, but Teddy felt that uneasiness begin to dissolve.

"Well, hey," Teddy interjected as soon as there was an opening to cut ties, clapping his hands together, "guess we all better get up to the lake."

Ben followed right along with parting ways. "Yep, yep. Better get goin'. Pete and Carrie may even be there already. Hey, we'll see you guys up there."

After he was inside and buckled up, Teddy started the engine, put the Jeep into Drive but quickly braked after the tires rolled about a foot. He turned to Denna with an accusatory stare and flared his nostrils with a sigh.

"What?" Denna said, no idea what she had done wrong.

Teddy wasn't even subtle about his gloating.

"I told you they would ask!"

2:54 p.m.

"He told you they're not vaccinated?" Concurrent with this question, Kelsey felt the distaste of dread bloom as a thick slab in her throat. By the way her husband dropped himself into the driver's seat of their 4Runner and closed the door with such force, she knew something had put him in a mood.

"That's what he said." Ben's hands were flexing, kneading into the rubber coating over the steering wheel, knuckles protruding white. They pulled out of the Mirabito, the directions to the lake guiding them along Route 33 through the town. Teddy and Denna had yet to leave the pumps and follow. "They also haven't been wearing their masks, apparently. That's the gist I got."

"I'm sorry." Kelsey chewed on her bottom lip, knowing how sensitive her husband was to other people's choices regarding the pandemic, especially if he believed them to be careless. She started dabbing and scrolling away on her phone. "I feel like when Denna first mentioned this lake house idea someone—maybe it was Carrie?—asked if everyone got their shot, and I thought Denna said they did."

Perusing the thread in their group chat that went back several months to the onset of summer in late June, Kelsey didn't locate any such message, dawning on her now as a possible faulty memory. The other pairing of friends coming along on this trip, Carrie and Pete Turnbull, had, unprompted, mentioned their inoculations early with the intent of setting minds at ease when agreeing to the idea of a cookout and overnight stay at Echo Lake. But they had never inquired about the vaccine status of the others. Furthermore, Kelsey was taken aback upon realizing she'd never offered up her and Ben getting their COVID shots into the running chat. This lapse would surely upset her husband.

"You find anything?" Ben asked. "Did she say they got their shots when they really didn't?"

Kelsey couldn't bring herself to admit the extent of her errors. Her husband didn't do social media, so he was only aware of what appeared in the group chat via her being the informant. She couldn't outright lie, but detailing the scope of her gross carelessness would grant him immediate cause to be upset with her. And she didn't need that right now.

"I guess I thought she did, but it's not here. Maybe it was in a text? I'll check through those."

Branching off Route 33 was a left turn onto Bass Lane, a straight and narrow road fallen to disrepair. The split asphalt had deteriorated to crumbled chunks of pavement and loose stones along its edges. This neglected pathway, littered with small, snapped branches and tumbling leaves, permeated a sea of trees through a crude natural archway of full branches reaching over. According to the directions on Ben's phone, their destination at the lake was eight-tenths of a mile down through the mass of these woods. When he glanced in the rearview and didn't spot the Meers's Jeep coming up the road behind them, he made a snap decision to pull over onto the shoulder and shift the 4Runner into Park.

"Do we stay, you think? Do we go home?"

"Uh…" Kelsey didn't know how to answer.

"I mean, we're vaccinated, so are Pete and Carrie you said, but… I know it's not likely we could get it, especially me again, the numbers are the lowest they've been since the beginning and still falling, but it's still a risk, a risk for my mother and the kids—all of us." He growled a long strain of frustration. "Why do some people have to be so fucking irresponsible? I don't get it."

Kelsey didn't have any answers for this either but knew her husband wasn't looking for a solution. He needed to vent. And for the first time in a while, he wasn't venting about her—her tendency to apply so much focus on work, her lack of energy or drive at home—or about how they were dropping the ball when it came to the communication in their marriage. In this newest matter, she wasn't the focus of his frustrations. A nice change in scenery, for sure.

Neurotically, Ben kept eyeing the different mirrors for the Meers coming up on them. He wanted to make a decision before they appeared. "So shitty of them to be the ones who propose this kind of thing and then turn out to be the only ones to not get the shot."

An angry tick, he started knocking the side of his right hand, pulled tight in a fist, progressively harder on the leather-padded armrest.

"It's people with that kind of thinking who got us where we were and why we couldn't get past this pandemic any quicker. They don't think about anyone but themselves except for those who are stupid and like-minded—"

His ranting ceased when Kelsey laid a cool, calm hand over his tapping fist. His hand turned steady.

Ben looked at his wife. In her eyes, without her saying a word, he discovered his own wrongdoing.

"I was gonna keep talking if you didn't stop me."

"I know."

"I need to just chill out and let this go."

"Uh-huh."

Taking a slow, deep breath and letting the air out in one audible expression of relief, Ben realized he was sitting pitched forward—back, neck, and shoulder muscles rigid and knotted. At his wife's quiet behest that was all in a look, he corrected his posture, bringing himself to relax by slowly reclining back into the seat, his back contouring to the soft but firm ridges and lumbar supports, sinking against the cool leather padding. Changing his position and focusing on his breathing was like taking pressure off a pinched nerve and allowing the blood to flow freely. Almost immediately he felt better, though not entirely at ease.

"I know you're upset," said Kelsey. "I know this means a lot to you. And because of that, it means a lot to me, too. I don't like seeing you so upset and bothered. I want you to have a good time. I want *us* to have a good time. I want tonight to be good for us."

She gave his fist—his motionless and weakening fist—a firm squeeze.

"And because of all that," she continued, "I do think we should stay."

Ben was moved by the conviction in her voice, in her unwavering gaze. Though not necessarily sold. "Yeah?"

Another squeeze of his hand. The fist relinquished.

"Yeah. Remember? When I said you were right before? We need to stay."

Ben smiled, though she could see how reluctant that smile was in appearing.

In the rearview came the Meers's Jeep on approach. Ben gathered himself, outputting enough sunny pleasantness that his previous irritations would be undetectable to those outside their vehicle. Kelsey would be the first to attest that her husband's true emotions never deviated so fast. On the inside he was surely still wound up and stewing, blood roiling like an angry ocean. She was tense just knowing how he really felt. They both needed to remember what was at stake.

They needed this.

They needed to get out of the house.

They needed time with other adults.

They needed time with each other.

Normalcy.

The overnight stay at the lake also prolonged any action taken toward their separation. A mutually agreed upon separation, yes, but *agree* was such a flimsy term when taking into account the flared and frayed emotions after an hour or so of bickering (and trying not to wake the kids during said bickering) the night before about how best to work through the string of disagreements and communication problems they'd been having of late.

Kelsey wished she could have gotten a do-over. She wouldn't have been so hasty to agree to a response of separation that, in hindsight, came out of impulsiveness. A desperation she could admit to on her part to find and have an answer. A tangible shake-up of their world.

But would Ben want something different if given a do-over, or did he really mean what he said?

She wanted to ask.

She wanted to know what he was thinking.

The man she'd married wouldn't want to be apart.

So, why was this happening?

"Hey, you guys all right?"

The Meers had pulled up alongside, with Teddy calling across the way through their rolled-down passenger window. In turn, Ben pressed the switch to put down his own window.

"Guys okay?" Teddy asked again, unaware of it being a severely loaded question.

"Oh, yeah," said Ben, stating the lie nonchalantly. "The directions on my phone crapped out. Looks like we lost the signal—kind of spotty up here. Wasn't sure if we were supposed to take this left or the next one."

"Yeah, it's this one," Denna answered, checking her directions. "Then it's about a mile down this road. Take a left at the fork. Place shows up on the right—the first one, number eleven, Bass Lane."

"You wanna follow?" Teddy offered.

"I think we got it," Ben said.

The windows went up, and Teddy pulled left to cut across the lane, the Meers taking the decaying road through the archway of trees into the thicket of woods.

"I think we'll be all right." With this same conviction and a careful choice in words (*we'll be all right* versus saying *it will be all right*), Kelsey tried to reassure her husband. "We'll be outside most of the time, so the fresh air will help. We can take the rowboat out or go for a long walk so we're not always near them. Plus, we don't have to sleep inside if we're worried about them. We can take our sleeping bags outside under the stars if we want to."

She was hoping to incite a spark of positivity, hoping to see and hear some glimmer of optimism mirrored back from her husband. A semblance of connection. Reconnection. Instead, when Ben shifted the 4Runner into Drive and spun the steering wheel all the way left, the sentiments he relayed before peeling off the shoulder to follow were both glum and ominous.

"Let's hope those aren't famous last words."

Kelsey realized at this point she was going to have to relinquish expectations and go along for the ride. Whatever came from their evening and the subsequent overnight at the lake house would be what it was. An experience unto itself. Her chaotic spat of life with Ben was placed on pause, set to resume the next morning on their ride back home. And then…who knew. She had an idea but didn't dare speculate in the moment where they would pick things up. Would he remain determined to follow through with their time apart or were those emotions fleeting? How would the kids factor into their decision? They were still very young yet, but would a separation bring the children to take sides and villainize one of them in time? Was there a compromise to make where their lives wouldn't be so entirely upended?

Better to push those thoughts to the side, she figured. Focus on now, best as possible, and try to enjoy herself, best as she could. Best as she could hide from the others.

Though, now in the direction of their destination with only minutes to spare before the car ride would be over and the hexad of friends reunited after nearly two years apart, Kelsey didn't imagine it was a good omen to start on when they passed beyond the tree line into shadow and a slight onset pressure behind her eyes warned her of an emerging headache.

New York State Route 17-E
3:03 p.m.

With the needle of the odometer dialing toward eighty-five in a posted seventy, Pete Turnbull grit his teeth and swore under his breath, awaiting the worst when passing a state trooper parked in a turnaround. Having been pulled over a time or twelve for speeding in his forty-two years, Pete avoided touching the brakes and only stole quick glances in his mirrors to see if the patrol car had left its spot to pursue. Rather than press on the brakes for an immediate slowdown—an obvious admission of guilt—he let his foot off the gas, letting the Mazda leisurely decelerate on its own. At the very least he could feign ignorance. Could say he couldn't remember the last time he saw a posted speed limit sign. He also didn't turn his head when searching the mirrors, darting around with only his eyes. Too much movement revealed an anxious driver fully aware of breaking the law.

"I think we're okay…" he said with uneasiness, not wanting that guess to be a kiss of death. The two lanes in their wake remained empty. No flashing lights, no sirens. The trooper was either not paying attention, napping, filling out paperwork, or, just as likely, didn't care.

In the passenger seat his wife Carrie turned to look out the back window, letting out a held breath that was mostly relief. Pete caught the undertone of disapproval in her sigh that spoke directly to how often she thought he gambled too much with chance.

"I told you we don't need to race to get there. Kelsey said they just stopped for gas like five minutes ago. We certainly don't need *another* speeding ticket."

"I've gotta say, I'm feeling a little attacked right now," said Pete. "And by the way, that ticket was totally bogus. Guy nailed me for using the passing lane to go around a tractor trailer that wasn't even doing the limit. That's crap. That's exactly what the passing lane is for! It's because we were in PA and he saw the New York plates."

"You were also doing ninety," Carrie reminded.

"I…wanted to make sure we got around him much faster." Pete glanced sideways at his wife and saw she wasn't buying his lame excuse.

"Two hundred and twelve dollars for passing a truck that wasn't doing the limit. Just keep that in mind." Carrie once again looked out the back window to make sure the trooper wasn't in pursuit. "We got lucky he let you off the hook and didn't actually give you the ticket for speeding. He wrote it for something else."

Pete chuckled. "Failure to turn on my four-ways when pulled over. We didn't even know that was a thing!"

"Still, a much cheaper ticket and no points on your license."

"Oh, I paid in other ways," Pete grumbled with disdain. "Wasn't it two weeks cold in the bedroom?"

Carrie raised both pencil-enhanced eyebrows and let loose a zero-tolerance glare. "You get pulled over and given another two-hundred-dollar ticket, and it's going to be cold in the bedroom for the next month."

Pete cocked his head at the thought. "I must be doing something wrong if I'm paying a whole lot of money and not getting some."

"Ha," retorted Carrie, who wasn't expressing amusement.

With the hand of the odometer now pointing at seventy-two, Pete thought it best not to push his luck. "Anyway, I wouldn't feel like we had to race if my stupid sister could have been on time. We told her we wanted to leave by one thirty and that we wanted to be gone before Ava woke from her nap."

"You know Becky," Carrie said, checking the status of a small zit on the underside of her chin in the visor mirror. "She's always on her own schedule." Locating then pinching the tiny red bump between the manicured nails of her index fingers to force the white head to the surface, she winced at the pop that stung for only a second. She snatched a tissue from her purse and dabbed the clear ooze and dot of blood off her chin. Her husband ignored this grotesque handling of her skin imperfection. He was too busy digging something out of his left nostril that she, in turn, chose to ignore.

"I just wish she could be more considerate," said Pete. "More responsible. Especially if, one day, she wants to be a mother."

This comment induced an incredulous cackling out of Carrie. "I think your sister will become a nun before she ever becomes a mother."

"I don't know. Something's different with her lately. Maybe it's that new guy she's been seeing. She jumped at wanting to watch Ava when I asked my parents to do it."

To further her point, Carrie added, "Between your other sister's now three-year-old and Ava turning two in December, Becky's never once even changed a diaper."

"If you didn't trust her to watch Ava, then why did you agree?"

Carrie folded her arms with a smug look on her face. "I totally expect that once your sister's in over her head, she'll call your parents to come help. And you know them. They'll drop everything and run right on over to the rescue."

"God, you're devious." Pete was sort of impressed—enough that he weirdly felt a little tingling, a little stirring in his stomach and materializing lower, between his legs began a bit of a stiffening, turned on by his wife's striking conviction. "You're actually looking forward to Becky falling on her face."

To this, Carrie gave a shrug of indifference. "If it happens, it happens."

"Cool to know you're willing to sacrifice our only child to prove you're right." Pete then shook his head, dumbfounded. "I have no idea why this whole setup is giving me such a boner right now."

With that same confidence, his wife applied a gentle pat and rub to his upper thigh. "I suggest you don't get a speeding ticket then."

Pete was determined to keep the odometer pointing below seventy-five.

Carrie's phone dinged with the arrival of a text.

"Denna says they're almost there. Wondering how far away we are. Looks like they ran into Kelsey and Ben at a gas station and things were a little awkward."

Hearing Denna's name sparked a further reaction through Pete. He became afflicted with a twitching and gurgle in his stomach, a flash of heat through his ears, and a slight prickling that flared over his shoulders and arms.

In tandem with his wife reading her friend's message, he pictured Denna—her much shorter frame than his six-foot-two. Her petite body and ghostly pale complexion. Her piercing and flecked emerald eyes. The smattering of freckles around her nose. In no way did he understand the attraction that bewitched him. He adored his wife. Was ashamed of his lusting for another woman. Personality wise, he and Denna didn't match up at all. They didn't know each other beyond the surface level. They were simply friends by association—acquaintances, really. In the six years he had been with Carrie, he may have only spoken a few sentences to Denna here and there, nothing deep or thought-provoking. He did think her husband was funny though.

"Probably *was* awkward," he said. "It's been more than a minute since we've all seen each other. It's like we're all learning how to act normal around other people again."

"So, maybe you shouldn't be digging in your nose then?" Carrie suggested.

Pete smirked. "Whatever you say, Miss Pimple Popper."

He wondered what he would feel when the anticipation was over and he actually saw Denna again, in the flesh. Soft flesh the tint of smooth half-and-half creamer. Maybe more would be on display than usual if everyone else brought their swimsuits to the lake.

These thoughts, intrusively bleeding through filters that upheld his morals, felt wrong. But no one could ever read his thoughts and know…

Carrie's phone dinged.

"And here's Kelsey." She took a moment to read. "She says Teddy told Ben they didn't get the vaccine and haven't been wearing their masks when going out." Carrie's eyes widened. "Yikes. Ben's probably pissed."

"Dude's always been wound up tight about this whole COVID thing. I mean I get it, but we always figured Denna and Teddy weren't getting the shot. Ben can't be all that surprised."

Carrie typed back a response to Kelsey that was simply the shocked emoji. She didn't want to insert herself into a brewing situation. "Yeah, but Ben and Kelsey have been, like, super careful this whole time. I know she jumped on the chance to get the shot when teachers were eligible. She was probably first in line."

"With you right behind her," Pete teased, knowing Carrie had been just as concerned about getting her inoculation when it looked like the opportunity was coming around.

"Oh, please," Carrie said with a chuckle. "Don't you go acting like you weren't wishing you worked in schools so you could have gotten it when we did."

"Because I want everything back to normal as quickly as possible," Pete said in his defense. "This craziness needs to be over. Once I could get it, I did. I gladly did my part. If this whole road to the lake house was covered in mousetraps, I'd army crawl the rest of the way butt-ass naked if it meant tomorrow the world was back to the way it used to be."

"I don't think anyone will be asking that of you," Carrie said, plunking her phone into the pocket near the handle on the passenger door, "but amen to that."

He sneered at the thought of conflict spoiling their evening. "I just hope no one talks about any of that stuff while we're together."

"Me either." Carrie reclined in her seat, tossing her bare feet up on the dash. "That will totally spoil this whole overnight, and we *need* this. A night away with no kiddo waking us up early—I fully plan to tip a few back and drunk-sleep soundly right on through to nine or ten in the morning."

"I hear you there," Pete said. "Maybe once the alcohol starts flowing, everyone will relax and we can all cut loose a little bit."

"I'm sorry, is it the nineties? When's the last time you heard somebody say *cut loose*?" His wife laughed. "Most of us work in education—how wild do you think it's going to get? Like we'll all be playing strip poker and doing wife swaps? Hey, since Denna didn't get her injection, maybe you can give one to her."

Carrie entertained herself to the point her cackling worked into hysterics.

"Whoa, whoa," said Pete, cutting her off right there. "Way to quickly make it all weird. That's not what I meant, and you know it." Though now the thought was painting vivid pictures all over his mental canvas. "Maybe—*maybe*—we could all play Monopoly or Scrabble, perhaps Stratego if anyone else knows how to play, but that's about as *cutting loose* as I was thinking."

That all sounded quite dull, but luckily for Pete, he could pull off dull with a bit of self-deprecating charm.

Carrie's face warmed with a wry smile. "Is that so?"

By her leading inquiry, Pete knew what his wife was pointing out. The stiffening at the front of his shorts, brought on from so many illicit mental snapshots inspired by her pairing him and Denna and the innuendo of *injecting* in the same suggestion. It was a harmless joke by his wife who didn't know the unfortunate and complicated and conflicting emotions that troubled him, resulting in an unfortunate erection (if there ever was a thing).

"That's entirely on you," he said, handing off culpability like it were a hot potato. "You're talking about strip poker and sleeping with people and we have a toddler who has ESP or something—she knows every time I try to make a move, wakes up, and calls for you because she wants you to snuggle her back to sleep. I can't help it. Anything at this point can set this thing off."

Carrie decided to test that theory by unbuckling her seat belt and running a hand gently over the newly formed tent reshaping the center of her husband's lap. "Anything?"

Pete swallowed. "What? Here? Right now? I'm trying not to get a ticket, remember?"

"No kid around to spoil the moment." Carrie slid two fingers beneath the flap and dragged the slider of his zipper down the chain, opening the mouth. She reached inside, going as deep as her wrist to get a handful of her husband, bringing him out into the light. "Just keep your eyes on the road. And stay below seventy-five."

With no intent to argue, and his life firmly in her hands, Pete released a wobbly breath, his lips quivering into a smile. "Y-yes, ma'am."

A sign came up on the roadside their friends had already passed, indicating they were fifteen miles from the town of Woodstock.

The needle of the odometer wavered but held steady within the limits.

3:06 p.m.

Kelsey checked her phone's home screen again when she realized she hadn't heard back from Carrie, noticing now the carrier's name and the bars of signal strength had vanished and been replaced by the words *No Service*.

Her headache was worsening. Dull pressure settled in, knitted stiff above her eyebrows. She supposed the drop in signal and emergence of tension in her head were byproducts of the woods—the thick presence of dominating tree growth cutting off the output of any nearby cell towers and the floating atmosphere of microscopic dust and allergens trapped beneath the leafy canopy that obscured the clouding sky entering their car through the open vents. The first weekend of September was a common time for allergy flare-ups—the commencement of seasonal changeover underway with the arrival of ragweed, with leaves and grass beginning to wither and mold. Kelsey was sensitive to it all and had forgotten to take her allergy medicine.

"Looks like the signal will be spotty," she said, pinching and pressing on various pressure points across her brow and down the sides of her face, trying like a pianist to dial in the right combination of notes to stave off the deepening ache. She resigned herself to shut her eyes and lay her head back after witnessing the return of a single bar's worth of reception. "I keep losing service."

Ben replied, "Not a big deal. We can always drive back out to the main road later when we check on the kids."

Though the crumbling and forsaken road wasn't designated by signage, he knew this to be Bass Lane from having previewed the directions. The narrow double lane they traveled along would eventually come to a fork about a mile in where he would be directed to veer left on a one-way.

But before they arrived at the fork, Ben slowed to an unexpected stop.

"Well, that's going to be a problem."

Kelsey opened her eyes. The diminishing headache resumed once the muted daylight was allowed back in to touch her corneas, forcing her to squint until her vision adjusted and the pressure relented. The pain had become low on the discomfort scale but was present enough to be an annoyance. Kelsey sensed—and kept hope—it was slowly, but surely, withering away.

"What's the matter?" she said before checking the scene out for herself.

Ahead of them on the road, Teddy and Denna's Wrangler had also come to a stop, red brake lights shining full. Out ahead of them a downed ash tree cut off their access to the rest of Bass Lane.

"Now what?" Kelsey asked.

Ben rubbed his chin and lower lip. There weren't many options to consider. The tall ash had fallen in such a way that it not only reached completely across the road but laid amongst the standing trees that were so close to the decrepit path the idea of skimming their vehicles past by driving along the shoulder wasn't a viable alternative.

Kelsey suggested, though wasn't assured, "Maybe we can move it?"

Tapping on the steering wheel, Ben didn't feel confident in this query given the tree's mass and considerable length. The uprooted base over twenty feet away was wedged between half a dozen of its upright comrades on the left, the crown was the same on the right. The trunk of the ash was as big around as a metal garbage can. Ben popped open the cover of the armrest and took out a black hard-shell glasses case.

"You have a headache, too?" Kelsey recognized the telltale sign. Her husband only ever wore his glasses for that very reason.

"I kinda feel one coming on, just above my eye." Ben took out the thick-framed pair of transition lenses and slipped them on his face. He pressed a red button on the dash to activate the vehicle's four-ways, warning anyone who might come up behind them on the road.

At the same time Ben and Kelsey stepped out of their vehicle to investigate, so did Teddy and Denna. Having already reconnected, the two men acknowledged each other with simple nods and pained frowns over their circumstances, approaching the downed ash running a diagonal angle across their path. The ladies exchanged pleasantries, with Kelsey quipping, "Girl, after all this time we've been stuck inside, how are you not pregnant yet?"

"Once again," Teddy interjected, "didn't I tell you they would ask?"

The four inspected the problem laid out before them.

"Probably came down in a storm," Denna said.

"How lucky for us," remarked Kelsey. "It's the only one down and, of course, right in the road."

Ben glanced around, noticing as well that no other trees lay on the floor of the woods. No others were leaning, nor had suffered obvious damage. All in the vicinity remained upright, their leaves closer to the tops whispering in a warm shot of breeze. "We had a storm on, what, Sunday? No way this has been here for almost a week. It would have been taken care of."

Teddy placed his foot on the trunk and gave a hearty shove, only to learn the hefty tree wasn't about to move in kind. Instead, Teddy ended up propelling himself back half a step on the road. "Probably just came down. Today…maybe last night. Could be that it's just old."

"I don't think so," said Denna. "It's not as big as some of the others. It's still a young tree. It definitely didn't fall last night or today."

Kelsey remarked proactively that she was no tree expert before asking, "How do you know that?"

"Look at the leaves. They're all dead."

In unison, Kelsey, Ben, and Teddy observed the top end of the splayed ash, where bending and snapped branches were mostly bare, the exceptions holding withered, browned leaves. Those that had loosened and dropped off lay curled up and flaking in pools of other browned or grayed leaves.

"What does that mean?" Kelsey wondered. Ben popped a leaf off the end of a twig, finding it so brittle it reduced to flakes and dust in his palm just by the little effort it took to pluck it free.

"It means all of the water inside the tree dried up," Denna said. "That doesn't just happen in a few hours or even overnight."

Aloud, Kelsey theorized, "Maybe it's been dead for a while and then it fell over? Aren't there invasive bugs that can kill a tree? Termites, you think?"

"I don't know about that either," Denna said. "It doesn't look like an unhealthy tree. The bark is mostly intact. Plus, it's the only one, but honestly…I don't know."

Ben broke in. "That's just it—we don't know. But it doesn't matter why or how it fell over. What matters is getting it out of the way."

Teddy shrugged. "Who do we call to remove a tree on the road—911?"

He caught a dirty look from his wife. "You don't call 911 for a tree."

"We don't have a signal here anyway," added Kelsey. "We'd have to drive back out to the main road if we wanted to make a call."

"We're about half a mile from the house," said Ben. A mosquito, or something that sounded like one, was whining incessantly by his ear. He swatted at it and connected hard with a resounding *thwack* on his neck which was already damp with sweat. His hand showed no sign of a dead insect. "We can either walk to the house and maybe find a chain saw or an ax or something there to help get this thing moved, or we drive back out toward town and get ahold of someone—a tree service."

"You think we're going to find a chain saw?" Kelsey asked. She slapped at the top of her exposed arm, feeling the pinch of an insect bite. Her hand, too, was devoid of a crushed insect cadaver.

"Lots of trees out here," said Denna. "I'm sure limbs come down all the time. My friend probably has something at the house that we can use. If not, maybe we can ask one of the neighbors."

"Especially if one of them is a serial killer," added Teddy. Again, no one laughed at his gallows brand of humor. Again, the smile quickly retreated from his face at the universal sight of dour, humorless glares stemming from the others. "Fine. Don't come crying to me when I turn out to be right."

Ben started back toward the parked vehicles, walking through a curtain of swarming gnats hanging as a shimmer in the air. "One thing's for sure—we're going to get eaten alive the longer we stand here debating what to do. I say we walk to the house and maybe take care of it ourselves. Who knows how long we might have to wait for someone else to come do it, especially on a weekend. Could take hours."

The others aligned into agreement. From their vehicles they grabbed their bags and their coolers to take along on the walk. Kelsey opened a side pocket on her overnight bag and dug out a bottle of bug spray to spritz herself down. She offered it to Ben, who doused his legs, arms, and the back of his sun-kissed neck.

"You guys want some?" She offered the spray to Denna and Teddy.

Denna examined the bottle. "Is it organic?"

Kelsey blinked, initially lost for words. Denna's newfound dedication to all-natural products with essential oils had lapsed her mind. She recalled now—at being asked about the spray—skimming Facebook one late evening while everyone was abiding by stay-at-home orders and seeing Denna's haughty post about no longer using products (as she put it) "that were full of chemical shit we can't even pronounce." Kelsey let it all slide when she responded. "It…keeps bugs away?"

"Should we leave the cars in the road or park them off to the side?" Teddy asked Ben while shouldering his pack.

"They should be fine here. We'll keep the flashers on." Ben pressed the lock button on his fob. The 4Runner's exterior lights blinked once, and the door locks engaged with a *beep* while the four-ways continued to flicker. "We won't be gone for long. Plus, it's not like anyone is getting through anyway. Maybe by the time we get back, Pete will be here to help out."

With everything they considered essential in hand, the foursome traversed over the obstacle that was the fallen ash and began the trek along the decaying road in the direction of their destination at the lakefront.

"You guys see the *Friday the 13th* remake?" Teddy asked. "The one where Jason sets traps for his victims? What if that tree being down is—"

The others answered in unison: *"Shut up, Teddy!"*

11 Bass Lane
Echo Lake, NY
3:31 p.m.

The exterior facade of the L-shaped ranch house was a hodgepodge of aesthetic design. From the left end going right, the front wall jutting out toward the road was composed of white panel board. The inward wall around the corner with the first of two plain red front doors was half stone composite, the other half white aluminum siding leading into the inside elbow. Red panel board made up the road-facing wall where the other front door was set. The rest of the face of the house, containing two white-framed windows, was once again stone composite. The collective mashing of exterior designs, Kelsey recognized, played a kind of visual homage to a similar style commonly found in Pennsylvania Dutch farmhouses.

On approach, Teddy whistled a long note, both impressed and staggered by the offbeat, inconsistent sight. To his wife he said, "Looks like your janitor friend had a hard time making up his mind."

Denna humored him with a cutesy smirk that was every bit as effective as flipping him the bird. "He told me when he bought the place that it looked exactly like this. Gives it character." She dug the front door keys lent to her out of a front pocket on the small army-green canvas bag slung across her front. "I like it."

"Certainly not a looker," Ben said of the house, "but I'm sure it's loaded with personality."

"Ironic," quipped Kelsey to her husband. "I said the same thing about you after our first date."

What she got from Ben in return was a dispassionate chuckle. In ordinary times, ragging on each other was a pastime he seemed perpetually primed for—all too glad and ready and willing to exchange verbal salvos for the sake of loving playfulness. With the recent developments (deterioration) in their marriage, however, there was just no readable desire from him to be cheeky with her. From Ben's perspective, he understood Kelsey was trying to maintain a front with their friends since the news hadn't yet broken, but even for the sake of keeping them in the dark a little bit longer, he didn't feel like playing along just for show. Faking it to make it was not his thing.

"I think that's John's van actually." Denna directed them to a windowless, beat-up red Dodge Ram parked in the medium growth of lawn on the far right of the house. The bald tires sat in a makeshift driveway that was born out of a pathway of flattened grass. The wraparound yard that opened up behind the lake house led to a sloped path down back where it narrowed to a small dock extending out about ten feet into the lakefront with a two-person paddleboat tied to a post. The back panel doors of the van stood open, as did the driver's side, but the vehicle appeared unoccupied. A gas push mower sat unmanned just a few yards away in the grass. A cutting trail had been started, leading toward the shallow slope that went down back, where the mower was stopped and abandoned.

Inspecting the mud-caked tire wells marred with rust beginning to spread over the body like some flesh-eating bacteria, Teddy kept his voice low in case Denna's friend happened to be in the back of the vehicle. "Your friend also drives a rusted-out, windowless van? This dude is shady as fuck."

"He is *not*," exclaimed Denna with a hiss in her tone. "He's been the head custodian at my school for over thirty years. The kids love him."

"Jesus," Kelsey chimed in. "He's a janitor at an elementary school driving a creepy-ass van and living in a weirdo-ass house out in the middle of nowhere? Dee, are you just now hearing all of this out loud for the first time?"

Denna was quick to correct. "He doesn't actually live here. This is just where he spends his summers."

"Glad that's straightened out," said Kelsey, not feeling one bit of her uneasiness smooth over.

Teddy chipped in, "This place is probably where he dumps the bodies."

Denna stomped her foot in the mangy grass. "There are no goddamn bodies!"

"Guys," said Ben, casual but cutting enough that the demand for their silence and attention was heeded. "I hate to break it to you, but you're not being as quiet as you think you are." He approached the back of the open van and peered inside. When he didn't see Denna's janitor friend inside, he shook his head, but something else nabbed his attention, causing Ben to set a knee on the red-carpeted interior floor of the van and climb halfway in.

"What is it?" Kelsey asked.

Teddy took two steps back toward the road. "If he brings out a suit made of human flesh, I am out."

After grabbing the grooved handle of what he spotted, Ben backed his way out. He brought with him a battery-operated chain saw that had been stashed in the back amongst other yard and maintenance equipment. He also managed to locate an extra battery pack.

"Oh," said Teddy, who was quietly relieved to not see blood spatter on the blade. "Well. That was easy."

Ben inspected a grimy white label with small, faded black type on the side of the Ryobi-branded saw. "Looks like if your friend is guilty of anything, it's that he's taking his lawn equipment from work." The sticker revealed the saw was the property of Saint Thomas Catholic School, 1 Aquinas Street, Serling Oaks, NY. The push mower parked nearby in the grass featured a similar label in rough shape on its deck.

Looking around to the others, Denna shrugged. "At least it wasn't bodies."

With the dull but intensifying pain radiating closer to the center of his forehead, throbbing behind and between his eyes, Ben pinched the very top of the bridge of his nose in a fruitless effort. The added pressure only localized the hurt, didn't diminish it. The fresher, cooler air blowing in off the lake wasn't doing enough to purge his headache. The persistent pain chewed away at his patience. "Let's just get it done."

"I'll go with you," Teddy offered. To which Ben only approved with a nod. Obviously, someone would have to tag along to drive the other vehicle left behind, much as Ben would just prefer going himself and hopefully, in solitude, clear his head of the gnawing drumbeat eroding his mood.

"We'll get everything situated here," Kelsey said. She was trying to be a comfort, reassuring, knowing her husband was worse off than he was letting on. When Ben got quiet or spoke to the point with a joyless tone, there was something bothering him. While her own headache had since dispelled enough to no longer be a burden, it was evident his had gotten worse. Which, she knew, compounded the other things on his mind. Their minds.

Ben adjusted his glasses, gave a jut of his chin in an "off we go" gesture then ventured up toward the road, chain saw and spare battery in hand. Teddy broke into a jog to catch up.

"See you in a minute," Denna called.

Teddy spun around on his heels and blew a kiss. "I won't say we'll be right back because, you know, that's like the number one mistake in a horror movie."

Being worn down by her husband's use of dark humor that was as unrelenting and continuous as ocean waves breaking on the coast, Denna relented with a roll of her eyes and a smile that he managed to earn through persistence (it wasn't the first thing he'd earned that way, truth be told). She returned the blown kiss, then with a lopsided grin she said to Kelsey, "Guess we get some girl time."

3:44 p.m.

Out of curiosity, she tried both of the front doors first and was surprised to find them locked. Denna used the key John gave her to let them in on the left side, her and Kelsey entering into a stocked pantry that was thickly warm. The silence within the house was also unexpected. She thought to hear John rummaging around somewhere, perhaps locating a container of extra gas for the push mower that was left unattended after only cutting a few yards of grass. But inside was as mute as a tomb.

"Hey, John?" Her voice carried through the small house. Past the pantry area was the kitchen, where the house cut right to the only bathroom before opening up into the shared dining and living room. The door to the bathroom stood open. Room dim. No one inside.

"Maybe he's visiting one of the neighbors," Kelsey said.

"Maybe." That wasn't out of the question, though Denna knew John to be the type who kept mostly to himself, though maybe he had a lot in common with those who inhabited the lake. When she was inquiring about the house rental after seeing a flyer in the teacher's lounge, John had talked her ear off about each of the eleven other residences at Echo Lake and their respective homeowners. Telling her which ones were nice, which ones were older couples, which ones had little kids, older kids, which ones would be drunk and blasting music and throwing their cans into the lake, and which ones would be lighting off fireworks at midnight and probably also be heavily inebriated.

"But they're all good people," John had told her, as if to waylay concerns. It was the most Denna had ever heard him talk. "Only two or three live up there all year round, and they like their peace and quiet. Those guys even have PO Boxes so the mail people don't have to come out. They all look out for each other. Nice little community we have up there in the summertime. Even if some get a little…rambunctious."

Kelsey set the coolers they lugged onto the small kitchen counter space and began unloading the drinks that ran a gamut of bottled IPAs to thin cans of hard lemonade seltzer, the meats and various salads, and the condiments to store in the mostly empty fridge. The leftover melting ice and reusable ice packs she dumped into the single bay sink. Denna pulled out the different packages of plastic utensils, Styrofoam plates and cups, and the napkins and paper towel rolls they brought in their bags. They both went about these preparatory tasks in the small kitchen space without much conversing. It was Denna who finally broke the ice in a way that demanded their unusual silence come to a definitive end.

"So, what's going on with you and Ben?"

Caught off guard by the brazenness of the question, Kelsey paused with a plastic bowl of a chef's salad in her hand while searching for space on a shelf in the fridge, which was a big tell. She couldn't be dismissive and be taken seriously, so she gave her best effort to be elusive.

"He said he was getting a headache."

Kelsey set the salad bowl inside next to a twelve-pack of hard lemonade and closed the fridge door to find, to her dismay, Denna no longer sifting through the packages of cups and plates and napkins but instead leaning her hip against the counter, arms folded, attention squared on her. Clearly, Denna wasn't going to be swayed, still interested in the trajectory of the conversation she had initiated.

"On the walk from the car you guys were like a mile apart," said Denna. A slight exaggeration, but the point was clear. "You didn't look at each other. Didn't hold hands. Not that you're obligated to hold hands, but it seems out of character for the two of you. Something's up. And I've gotta tell you, after all this time apart from you guys, I need something else to talk about that's not Teddy's work or Star Wars."

Initial fight-or-flight response told Kelsey to avoid responding. However, as the weight of the moment pressed down harder onto her shoulders and lingered, and because of the obligation she felt to her friend, and the seduction of shedding her burdens to a willing ear, once she got started, Kelsey found it easier to open the valve beyond just a trickle and let everything pent-up inside to come flowing out.

"Okay. Umm. We've had a hard run of things lately," Kelsey said. Already the pressure in her chest lightened up, her throat loosening—an encouragement that was making it easier to continue spilling the beans. "I mean, no marriage is perfect, right? At first, I think we thought it was just a snag everyone goes through. Except we kept getting hung up on small things."

Denna nodded. "Everyone having to stay at home at the same time and for so long…I think a lot of us expected it to feel like a vacation, but it turned out much harder than we thought. Plus, all the worries of getting sick—"

"Except this started about a week before everything shut down," Kelsey said. She went back into the fridge and fished out a couple of sweaty watermelon-flavored hard seltzers to continue fueling her confession. She handed one over to Denna, who accepted without protest. Without acknowledgment or ceremony, they popped the tabs and began pulling the bubbly sweetness tinged with a bit of strength to scratch their throats and warm their stomachs. "The Thursday before everything shut down, that day was hell with all of my classes—it was the first time I regretted leaving Saint Thomas with you and Carrie and getting the spot at the high school."

Kelsey expected Denna to interject and offer support, saying that moving out of the low-paying, no-benefit, no-retirement system that was the Catholic schools and finding a place in the Serling Oaks Central School District was more than just a good opportunity. That was the type of sentiment she had been showered with by all at Saint Thomas Elementary when news of her new appointment spread. But Denna just sipped from her can and remained content to listen.

"Ben also had a rough day at the middle school. I think many of his colleagues saw the writing on the wall—closing down, setting up virtual classrooms, figuring out how to teach remotely. Rumors were going around. Someone was saying the first cases were showing up in the county… I mean, for God's fucking sake, we have a big enough house and it felt like we had to hunker down in our master bedroom with the kids like some apocalypse was happening."

Kelsey took a long and anxious guzzling pull, sucking from the can opening, which resulted in a juicy lip-smack when her suction released. She wiped her lips clean before resuming. "We both came home absolutely fried. We had food to cook for dinner but decided, you know what? Fuck it. Let's take the kids to Chuck E. Cheese. Might be the last time we do anything before…you know, we couldn't. So we did. The twins had never been there, but Margaret had—she about exploded with joy when we pulled in."

In joyful remembrance, Kelsey couldn't hold back a smile. Even Denna, who had yet to experience happiness through the glowing excitement of her own child, showed a warmth and fondness for the experience being told.

"We basically had the place to ourselves. There was maybe one other family with just two kids. But it was so much fun. We took so many pictures of Margaret playing Whac-A-Mole, the boys riding floating bikes and clapping, having the time of their lives. When the night was over, the kids passed right out in their beds. Such a perfect evening after a shitty day."

That glimmering in Kelsey's expression began to fade, starting with her eyes then slinking downward to erode her smile. She took a drink, a modest one this time. The seltzer provided another soothing scratch to her throat, which felt to be thickening and closing up with the apprehension of what continuation of the story she was about to share next. Perhaps even the introduction of alcohol couldn't completely tear down the walls of her reluctance, but since she'd already started, she pushed to finish.

"You would think a loving, happily married couple would take advantage of such a night. Make some part of it for them, together. Or at least try." Kelsey shook her head, already feeling disgust before speaking the truth. "Ben started reading work emails on his phone, and I did the same. We fell into the same trap we'd been falling into. We didn't even talk, not anything that wasn't work related or about the stupid pandemic. He fell asleep in the recliner and I on the couch. I woke up around midnight and went to bed by myself. He never came up. Didn't wake up until the next morning."

She blinked, hoping to keep a few forming tears at bay. Taking a drink of the seltzer helped in that way at least.

"We did this amazing night for the kids and for the five of us, but nothing for just him and me. That's when I knew."

She wiped beneath her eyes and took a deep breath to compose herself. Denna set her empty can down on the counter then took two more full ones out of the fridge to share.

"What did you know?" Denna asked.

Kelsey sniffled. "That something was wrong with my marriage."

They both cracked open the hard seltzers and set about draining them.

"Every marriage goes through its slow years," said Denna while wiping her bottom lip. "Maybe that's all this is. Not every sour experience means it's the end of anything. It also could be nothing at all. So what if you had one quiet night? It's okay to not have something to say all of the time. Doesn't mean you don't have a healthy marriage. You were being real with each other—you were exhausted. In moments when we're hardest on ourselves, it's easy to see nothing as something."

"Yeah… I don't know." After emptying almost two twelve-ounce alcoholic beverages in a matter of a few minutes, Kelsey wiped away the brewing tears and felt the welcoming sensation of warm carbonation fizzing through her head and belly. Hearing her own plight out loud put things into a better perspective. Maybe Denna was right. Maybe. Maybe she was looking too hard to see their situations as more than they were. Would have come across more insightful and genuine had Denna not sounded like she was just trying to cheer Kelsey up, but they hadn't been together in a while so Kelsey gave her a pass.

Kelsey also decided to turn the tables—another by-product of twenty-four ounces of alcohol swimming in her system.

"What about your marriage?" she point-blank asked Denna. "Thought you guys were trying to have kids?"

Denna didn't seem at all bothered by Kelsey's own taking the initiative of cutting right to the gist. "Teddy still wants kids."

She finished the rest of her second can.

Kelsey persisted, catching the selective wording. "What about you?"

Now Kelsey realized the vulnerability, the Achilles' heel. That subtle reaction. Denna's eyeline drifted away then back again.

"I do." But even Denna knew she wasn't convincing. "Someday."

"We're getting to the end of our thirties. What are you guys waiting for?"

Denna looked like she didn't know what to do with her hands, so she picked up one of the empty Truly cans standing beside her on the counter and fumbled with it. Using it as a fidget, a means of distracting her jangled nerves. "It's not us. It's me. I've…uh…I stayed on the pill."

"What?" The revelation of why Denna had such a hard time sharing this came instantly to Kelsey, just as quickly pouring out of her mouth before it was a composed thought. "And Teddy doesn't know."

"He used to think it was just taking a long time. Now I think he's wondering if there's something wrong with one of us. That we can't get pregnant."

Kelsey folded her arms, wanting to also fidget with something but not look like she was copying her friend during an uncomfortable moment. "But why?"

Setting the can back down on the counter, Denna walked into the living room area. Kelsey followed. After slipping off her Converse on the braided wool rug beneath the coffee table, Denna sat cross-legged on the middle cushion of the blue plush couch. She picked at the chipping black paint on her toenails as she spoke. Kelsey opted to leave the white-and-burgundy-striped love seat unoccupied and sit on the floor across from her, absently running the fingers of her right hand over the divots and along the grooves in the rustic table that was riddled with the scars of moisture rings of varied sizes from different instances in its time. With her left hand she fiddled with the knots of the woven, blue area rug beneath the table.

"Teddy's going to lose his job," Denna said.

"I'm sorry."

"It hasn't happened yet, but it will. It's been a matter of time since the shutdown. I think he wanted to believe things would get better with the reopening, but…"

Kelsey frowned, hoping to convey her understanding and her sympathy and not wanting to undercut Denna's venting by offering pities.

"Not that he was making fantastic money at TechWorld," said Denna, working on scratching and lifting away a large chip of loosened paint from her big toe as a single piece, "but I can't afford to support us on a Catholic school teacher's salary. You know how that is."

Again, Kelsey nodded, quite familiar with that particular financial conundrum indeed.

"We can't raise a family on thirty-two thousand a year. Thirty-two *before* taxes!"

"A lot of people do it, though," said Kelsey, trying to be supportive, though she realized afterward she hadn't pinpointed the real problem hanging ominously over her friend like a massive thundercloud. It wasn't about the money. "Where will Teddy go if he gets laid off?"

Denna immediately relinquished scraping the paint off her toenails. "That's just it—I don't know. He doesn't have a plan. He never does. He likes to think things just work out in their own time and in their own way, but… but I can't be like that. I can't bring a child into this. I can't make it up as we go. He's just… He's gotta grow up."

"Have you told him any of this?"

Seeming helpless, Denna sank back into the couch. "Dozens of times it feels."

Kelsey attempted to consider options that would be of any help to her friend, but her brain was treading water in the hazy pool of alcohol; it was easier to conjure a solution that was all "well, fuck him then" rather than anything practical and not so dismissive and confrontational. Still, though, fuck him then. Rather, what came over her instead, and she relaxed into it (floating on her back in this pool of alcohol), was a strange, fizzy warmth of familiarity. She had been here, countless times, with her friends—pouring over their problems, sometimes under the indulgence, always honest and clear. Where lamenting one's spouse or partner opened the speaker up to criticism (because didn't their complaining about the person they chose also reveal a flaw in their own decision-making skills?), these talks always remained judgment-free. Slipping back into these old conversations that were more about confiding in friendships offered another glimpse of life before the pandemic. One Kelsey was more than happy to return to living. At this moment, in this small house on the shore of Echo Lake, she didn't give a shit that Denna wasn't vaccinated. She was glad to have her friend in company.

Kelsey breathed a loud, exclamatory sigh that wasn't composed of or riddled with frustration and distress as its key ingredients, but one that also relayed her contentment. They may both have been facing some hard times at home, and answers weren't going to be easy to come by (if the truth was out there at all to find, or maybe they'd just have to continue to ride out their respective situations and hope for the best), however, they had this moment. This moment co-shared to commiserate and begin to reconnect after so much lost time in a divided, plagued world.

"You know what I think we need?"

"What's that?" said Denna.

Pressing both palms into the weathered coffee tabletop, Kelsey pushed herself to her feet. Warm fizzies shot up to her brain. "Another drink."

Kelsey held out an inviting hand. Denna accepted it, and they made their way back to the refrigerator.

After careful deliberation, Denna chose and popped the tab on a can of hard peach lemonade. "You think the boys are also talking about all this crap going on?"

For her next beverage, Kelsey decided on the hard watermelon. She sipped, felt the sparkles on her tongue, the bubbles swimming through her head, and found that to be a good choice. "Much as they would never admit it to us, I'm sure they're pouring their little hearts out to each other right now."

3:58 p.m.

"Dude, I'm telling you right now—pickles absolutely go on a pizza."

Coming to an abrupt stop in the middle of Bass Lane, Ben cut a bewildered, nose-curling cringe as if gathering auditory and olfactory evidence of a heinous, noxious fart drifting past and sledgehammering him in the face. "And I'm telling you, that sounds *absolutely* disgusting."

Mouth unhinging, dropping agape, it was Teddy now looking taken aback, as if his feelings had just been assaulted. "How so, dude? Have you even tried it?"

"*Dude.* I literally have never even heard of it until about twelve seconds ago when you brought it up," said Ben, who, despite the unusualness of their ongoing conversation regarding pizza toppings that sprung out of nowhere, had managed to let slip from his mind the whole aggravating issue he had with Teddy being unvaccinated. Chalk that up to the many years of bonding and friendship in a pre-pandemic world they had under their belts. In this wilderness, without any reminders of the world that was actually suffering from spreading illness and rising rates of death in all age categories, they were now back to the simplicity of being just two friends having their normal, however peculiar, conversation. Like the good old days, so goes the saying. "I like my pizzas plain. Maybe double cheese, maybe some pepperoni or sausage. Once in a while a sprinkling of peppers and onions, but that's about it."

"How very missionary position of you," said Teddy in a remark about all of that dullness as they resumed walking the stretch of decrepit road. He was starving to explain in a breathless rant how mouthwateringly fantastic a good dill pickle being sliced up in medallions and spread over a prebaked pizza pie was even if he never convinced Ben of this fact. Just talking, filling the quiet of their surroundings with banter, was a happy place to be. "I was once very closed-minded like you. But then Denna came home from work saying some of the teachers pitched in to get a couple sheet pizzas for the staff and someone asked for pickles as a topping. She thought it sounded gross—like you—and she thought she'd hate it—also like you—but then she tried it and came home saying how great it was. Even I was a skeptic at first, but then you know what?"

"You tried it?"

"I tried it—and freaking loved it."

"That is such a great story. I hope you guys get a lot for the rights—can't wait to see the film version. I'll probably wait to watch it on streaming though."

"Goodness." Teddy touched his chest as if he'd been on the receiving end of a sucker punch. "I do think one of us here needs to get laid more often and—*spoiler*—it isn't me."

Ben chuckled but didn't even bother opening that jack-in-the-box. He would discuss anything with Teddy at the moment: pizza toppings, the weather, the supposed impossibility for someone to lick their own elbow—hell, he'd go as far as to bring up the whole vaccination thing—but absolutely no way was he going to engage in a conversation about getting laid. That particular doorway led to too many hallways.

When conversation didn't resume right away, from the side of the road Teddy picked up a long stick, twirling it and stabbing it in the air like a Jedi Knight would a lightsaber while humming a whirring sound through clenched teeth. "You think there are enough bugs out here?" He began swinging the stick, whilst still humming with his saber, at the gnats and mosquitos gathering in cloudy hazes around his head. "Because I'm not so sure."

As they forged ahead, beneath the leaves flapping, through unseen insects chittering and the call of cicadas rising, with the mosquitoes whining close to his ears, Ben realized that his headache had begun to subside. The pain hadn't completely vanished but was diminished enough to improve his mood. Much as he hadn't been looking forward to the company (especially a close encounter with the unvaccinated kind), it turned out the opportunity to mend some damaged fences with Teddy was a welcome distraction in its own right.

"You know how to use that thing, by the way?" Teddy asked about the chain saw.

"No idea," Ben admitted. "I'm just really going to try not to lose any limbs with this thing."

"Solid plan." Teddy whooshed his lightsaber once more then gave up in his battle against the flocking insects.

When they arrived at the fallen ash, Ben inspected the chain saw and determined a pump switch on the topside of the curved handle was a safety that had to be depressed with his thumb while squeezing a trigger on the underside. The blade sputtered at first, then droned to blurring life after some priming. The saw, humming in Ben's hands, felt like a live animal to be contained.

Teddy offered an uneasy grin and thumbs-up for positive reinforcement then gave a wide berth, stepping far to the side. Before lowering the running blade to meet the splayed ash, Ben shoved his glasses all the way up to protect his eyes. Mentally, he prepared himself not to fuck this all up in front of his friend and have to leave Echo Lake in an ambulance with some part of him being kept in a cooler on ice.

He sucked in a breath and held it, lining up a cut down the middle. Operating out of an abundance of caution, Ben held the whirring saw as far away from his body as his taut arms would extend, hoping to cancel any chance for a mistake that would leave him maimed. Ben white-knuckled the grip, expecting a little kickback.

The blade sunk through the ridges of the bark as if the tree was made of warm butter. Even going slow, the chain saw chewed through the log without effort. Straining under the pressure, the last bit of the ash trunk snapped off, startling Ben back a bunch of steps to where he nearly let go of the saw as half of the tree dropped to the decrepit pavement. Feeling more comfortable (and manly!) wielding the tool, Ben moved to both shoulders of Bass Lane and made incisions that severed the trunk ends reaching over the road. When finished, Teddy helped roll the debris off to the sides.

"Nicely done," said Teddy.

"Thanks."

They stood admiring the completed work.

"I think we deserve a beer for this," Teddy added.

"Still so strange," said Ben. "This tree had to be down for days, if not longer. And no one came by?"

Teddy didn't have an answer to that. Could only shake his head as the truth was a guess at best. "It's out of the way now. You earned your 'man card' for today."

Ben held up the trusty saw in a victorious salute. "Guess we should get back. I think you're right—we've earned a beer or two."

As they got to their respective vehicles occupying the road, Ben set the chain saw and spare battery on the floor of the back seat of the 4Runner.

"Oh, hey," Teddy called out from beside his Wrangler, "I think I figured out a pizza topping we can both agree on."

"Yeah? What's that?"

"Green olives."

One foot up on the runner, Ben leaned against the open driver's side door, frowning. "You're just trying to fuck with me now, aren't you?"

A triplicate of car horn blasts directed their attention to a black Mazda 6 rolling up behind them. The front driver's side window slid down, and Pete Turnbull stuck his head out.

"Hey, losers, what's the holdup?"

"Oh, look who finally decided to show," said Ben.

"Right on time for him," Teddy chimed in. "The hard work's already done."

Teddy climbed into the Jeep, switched off the flashing hazard lights, and started up the engine to lead the way along the now unobstructed road. Ben followed. Pete and Carrie completed their convoy. The tires crunched over dead leaves and small sticks left in the wake of the fallen ash.

Along the short drive back to the lake house, Ben felt the nagging headache begin its renewal.

4:37 p.m.

Using a rock the size of his fist that he sourced from the bed of dried mud at the lakefront, Pete hammered down the last stake to secure the right-side pole holding up the badminton net. Teddy, using both racquets to juggle the birdie in the air, had found the game tucked inside the lake house's only closet that was set by the back door. Ben, meanwhile, resigned himself to slouching in a camp chair. He'd finally given in, believing the sharp pulse at the front of his skull wasn't going to leave on its own, and asked if any of the ladies had Tylenol or ibuprofen in their purses. Thankfully, Carrie had Midol. The takeaway: beggars can't be choosers.

Mercifully, Pete finished his banging on the head of the stakes. Each clanging impact with the rock had made Ben want to skewer a fork between his eyes.

"It's gorgeous out here," said Pete. "How'd Denna find this place?"

Teddy scooped the fallen birdie off the ground and resumed trying to keep it in the air. "Uh, the short of it is: creepy janitor at her school owns the place and was renting it out."

"Cool. And what's with the sex predator van parked out front?"

Without picking up his head, Ben uttered, "Also belongs to creepy janitor. Who may come back at some point to cut the grass." Every spoken word rang in his ears, adding to the localized pressure pinging from the center of his brow. The only comfort he could find waiting for the pain reliever to kick in was keeping his eyes closed, head reclined against the nylon backing of the foldout chair in the dancing shade.

He listened to the irregular swats and grunts and "oh shits" that made up the duration of the guys' badminton game. Every so often there was a bit of chatter, a ripping belch that was the result of one of them sucking down their beers too fast, a soft splash from the lake, a rustling of leaves, a crowing note from a bird, a heavy buzz of an investigating bumblebee. The gentle breeze that occasionally swept through the grounds brought the aroma of mud and water. But in reaching out, Ben couldn't locate any sounds related to people beyond their little group. On such a picturesque and pleasant late summer's day, it was strange that the six of them seemed to be alone at the lake.

Not one lawn mower was running.

Not one car or truck engine started up or passed by.

Not one dog barked.

Not one child cried out.

Not a single firework exploded.

Not that he was complaining.

I guess it's not an escape to paradise if you live here all the time, Ben considered. Likelihood was that the other permanent residents at the lake were either having quiet days inside their homes or had gone off on their own adventures. Maybe some went out for the day; maybe some took off to another locale for the weekend. He wondered if the lake dwellers, being a close-knit community as he had heard, ever ventured together to a secondary remote destination—a state park with camping grounds, perhaps?—to have their peace and solitude and community when outsiders would rent their homes to escape the noises of the towns and cities.

It was a good way to make some extra cash, at the very least.

A crunching *thud* on the ground near his chair was followed by an exasperated Teddy panting out, "Aw, I almost had it!" There was a hint of slurring to his words.

"Man, you really went for it," said an impressed Pete with an inebriated chuckle. "I would've let it drop, knowing my luck. I'd have broken an arm or something."

Ben despised missing out on the fun (and the drinking) he'd been so looking forward to for months (especially as a temporary getaway from the plights at home), but goddamn this headache. Kelsey had felt the beginnings of one just as they started following the length of Bass Lane into the woodlands surrounding the lake, but it didn't seem to have materialized like his had. And headaches didn't tend to incapacitate him like this one. It was a real fucking doozy. Enough that the slightest movement or the right sound or shine of light brought a heartbeat of agony pulsing through the pressure points in his face and radiating to the fillings in his back teeth.

The screen door screeched open, and the wives stepped out of the house, walking around the highly competitive badminton game on their way down to the dock. Carrie reminded Pete not to hurt himself. They didn't need a trip to the hospital this weekend. Pete responded with an affirmative, "Yessiree, ma'am." Denna gave Teddy the same reminder, adding TechWorld's health insurance sucked. Teddy replied, while breathless and continuing to volley the birdie, "Maybe I should see if Mirabito has better coverage."

"How're you doing?" asked Kelsey. Ben, eyes still closed, felt a solace in her shadow falling over him. When she laid a hand on the inside slope of his right shoulder, there was a pressing of real concern through the gentle massage of her fingers as she moved to the tightness along the side of his neck.

"Doing," was all Ben replied. Not worse, not better.

"We're going to go down by the lake. If you want, go in and lie on the couch for a bit. It's darker and quieter inside. Maybe that will help?"

"Yeah, maybe I'll do that." At this point, if bloodletting would resolve his pain, and the only way to accomplish that was with a rusted butter knife, Ben would not have completely shunned the thought.

"Okay." The hand of his wife gave a tender rub and pat to his chest before she departed to follow Denna and Carrie down to the lakeside.

Ben waited for the badminton game to pick up again with the guys crying out in tipsy excitement and gasping obscenities before slipping out of the chair and dragging his feet into the house. The first few moments of being upright cost him a spell of dizziness with hollow bells going off in his ears as the blood and different fluids got moving, which intensified the ache at the front of his head momentarily. All the way from the foldout chair to the couch, his eyes weren't able to pry open wider than a squint. He removed his glasses, laid them on the coffee table, and collapsed onto the firm and musty-smelling couch cushions. Once the world went still and settled, he found a position most comfortable. The back of his head, specifically the base of his skull, rested against the harder armrest. Stiff pressure against that exact spot seemed to help diminish the pain.

In the muted interior space of the lake house, thoughts navigated through webs of concerns and worries about the future and tasks to be done and how everyone was having a great time and weren't on their phones (which served as expensive paperweights for all the good they could do out here). Eventually, that focus honed in on his children. Margaret, Little Ben, and Ryan were likely taking every advantage of their babysitting grandma, but she allowed that to happen, if not outright invited it. There was no doubt his children were having the absolute time of their little lives. They were in good hands. Hands that would spoil them at every turn, but hands that would protect them and nurture them. They were loved.

He also thought of Kelsey outside, wondering if there was a way out of their separation. Did they need to go through with him moving out to learn how much they loved one another? Did the kids need to witness their family splitting up if the intention—the hope—was that time and space would bring them right back together? Or could they (as rational-thinking adults) learn to shift and refocus the priorities of their lives right now, this very moment, and make the concentrated effort to repair their bond, and make each other and the vows of their relationship—and not their dedication to their jobs—the most important?

The answers all seemed so simple. Right there within reach.

Clarity came through like a brisk wind on a hot day, dispersing all of Ben's worries, his doubts. He opened his eyes.

On top of this, his headache also vanished.

4:45 p.m.

Stepping up to the end of the shabby dock full of grayish, bending, and splintered boards, Carrie lowered herself to sit on the edge and dip a toe in the cool lake. She wasn't one for wading or swimming in such bodies where she couldn't see through to the bottom. The oily touch of the water, the slimy green residue on the surface near the shores, and the mystery of what tiny and slithery lake creatures and unknown quantity of sharp rocks were hidden beneath served as lifelong deterrents, even on the hottest of days. Her aunt Sheryl had owned a house on Echo Lake when she was young, and little Carrie would only admire the water, never venturing in when her cousins were all about taking turns jumping in off the dock. The scenery, however, from childhood through adulthood, couldn't be beat.

"Beautiful, isn't it?" Kelsey slipped off her flip-flops and took a seat next to Carrie. She added her own blue-nailed, well-pedicured feet to the lake. Their toes vanished into the murky water just inches below the surface.

"Even more than the beach," Carrie said. "For me anyway."

"Really? You don't care for the beach?"

Carrie looked out across the calm water bordered by woodland. The leaves fluttered. A few ripples popped up here and there over Echo Lake. The very edges lapped at the weedy banks and muddy shores. The lowering angle of the sun cast soft, saturating light. A resplendent, hypnotic view that reminded her of animated Windows screen savers that looped the same couple of seconds of serenity.

"I like the beach just fine. Mostly to look at and breathe the air. The atmosphere. The essence. But I hate sand—it gets absolutely everywhere—and I don't go into the water. I don't like going in where I can't see, especially when there are sudden drops. And I'm terrified of jellyfish."

"Gotcha. So you don't go into lakes either, I take it."

Carrie smiled. "I love a good swimming pool or Jacuzzi."

"Jacuzzi," echoed Denna, who occupied one of the Adirondack chairs back on solid ground just shy of the dock. She had her feet up and crossed on a matching ottoman. With her shades on she could have been zonked out for all they knew had she not spoken. "Now you're talking."

"But I'm a sucker for quiet and a view," said Carrie. "I'll definitely take this. Sorry Ben's not enjoying it so much."

"Just a headache," said Kelsey. "I had a little one, too, but not really feeling it anymore."

"That's funny." But Carrie wasn't being humorous. "Just a little while ago I started getting one. Right behind my eyes."

"Ben said he could feel it coming on as we were driving in. He has allergies though. Coming out here to the wilderness, we didn't think to pack any Claritin."

Carrie said, "I think mine's from the house. Stuffy as hell in there, and clearly, it hasn't been dusted or aired out in forever." She directed these critiques over her shoulder at Denna.

"Hey," Denna said sharply but in no way serious, "for the night this place cost us a hundred and fifty. Dust or no dust, you can't argue with that price. Anywhere else we could have gone Labor Day weekend would have easily doubled that."

Now Carrie's sense of humor played into her demeanor. "You get what you pay for."

Denna readjusted in the chair. Like Rafiki holding up a newborn from *The Lion King* for all the pride to see, she presented her newest can of whatever wine mixer she blindly picked that she didn't care what flavor it was because it was tasty and contained alcohol. "I paid to kick back, get sloshed, hang with you guys, and not have to think about finishing my classroom before Wednesday."

"Everyone ready for this coming year?" Kelsey asked, swirling her right foot around in the water, eyeing the floating specks and green scum on the lake's fringes. Her mood muted at the thought of the near future.

"Absolutely not." Carrie combed back her hair with her fingers and set her sunglasses on top to hold back her dark mane. "As much as I hated remote teaching, social distancing in the rooms, plastic barriers, sanitizing the desks and chairs over and over again, I'm not sure I'm ready to go right back to 'normal.'"

Kelsey agreed. "Most of my classes stayed at about fifty percent capacity throughout the whole year. Virtual teaching wasn't easy, but I'm not sure I'm ready to go from class sizes of five or six teenagers back to twenty."

"At least teenagers understood the rules we had to follow," Denna said. "Carrie and I had our hands full with the little ones."

Carrie added, "We were also in session five days a week. We didn't have 'remote' Wednesdays like you."

"Oh, you mean 'no work' Wednesdays?" added Denna with a knowing one-sided grin.

"Yeah, yeah, whatever, bitches," Kelsey said while flapping both hands like quacking ducks to indicate she was hearing nothing but nonsense.

The women started out snickering, but after Denna lost control and fizzies erupted out of her nostrils, they burst out with snorts and cackles of laughter that echoed across the lake bed. A shared laughter that spiraled into a near frenzy because it was powered by lowered inhibitions, infused by bubbly alcohol, and instigated by Denna's foamy nasal projections. Somewhere in the reeds a distant loon sang back at them, then came the layered cooing of a mourning dove. When the laughing fit was over, tears were wiped (as was Denna's nose) and smiles were shining bright. It was commented on and agreed upon how they missed this—being together—and how they needed to make their outings a more common event now that the world was getting itself back together.

Out of habit, phones eventually made their appearance, everyone forgetting the signal strength had been seesawing between slim and nil.

"It's almost five," said Carrie. "Anyone getting hungry? Should we start the grill?"

The thought of food put an audible rumble through Denna's belly. "I'll tell the boys."

Kelsey used the corner pylon to pull herself up. "I'll check on Ben."

Worked up into a full-blown sweat, Pete and Teddy had been volleying the game-winning point when Denna walked up to the net. "Guys ready to eat?"

The momentary glance her way, locking on to the sight of short shorts and the stalks of her pale legs with shapely calves, robbed Pete of all his focus on the task at hand. That millisecond lapse earned him the birdie being smashed into his chest and Teddy declaring victory.

"Loser cleans and mans the grill," Teddy said before they high-fived and said good game.

Pete watched Denna embrace and kiss her victorious and sweaty husband. A kiss, fueled by the same diminished inhibitions, that went a little deeper and longer than a quick display of public affection. That mysterious jealousy for Denna, another man's wife, burned in Pete's face. And when he tried to wrap his arms around Carrie with the hopes of experiencing some of the same affection, she balked at the sight of his darkened shirt.

"Ew, gross. You're all sweaty."

With a sigh, Pete wandered in the direction of the grill. He opened the lid, scratched off the caked-on debris best he could with the deteriorated wire brush laid on the grates, then repeated the ignition process with the knobs until finally a flame caught on the burners.

5:04 p.m.

Kelsey was hopeful her husband's headache had gone away, or at least slackened enough to be tolerable, when she stepped inside the back door of the lake house to find the couch in the living room area vacant. His glasses remained in solitaire on the dust-speckled coffee table. She inspected the lenses, blowing off the loose flakes of dust particles and wiping the smudges clean with the tail of her shirt. The bathroom door shut behind her, and she believed that to be Ben, so she waited to ask how he was feeling. Suffice to say, she was surprised when Teddy emerged minutes later to state a PSA, warning everyone they might want to let the room breathe a little before venturing inside.

"Who doesn't put windows in a bathroom?" Teddy asked rhetorically. No one fed into his attention-seeking except to answer him with grim expressions and grunts of disgust.

The next place Kelsey checked was the kitchen and connected pantry, but the only ones occupying the space were Denna and Carrie. Denna was taking the salads out of the fridge, shaking up the contents of the bowls, then removing their cling wrap tops. Carrie was unpacking hot dogs and burger patties and laying them on a wood cutting board to season with salt and pepper before taking them out to Pete to cook. They quickly noticed something amiss sketched on Kelsey's face and paused in their dinner prep.

"You didn't see Ben anywhere, did you?" Kelsey asked.

They both said no, hadn't seen him. Kelsey considered that he might've stepped out front for some air. But when she checked the front yard, there was no one to be seen.

"Not out here?" Carrie asked, coming up behind her in the pantry doorway that gave out to the front of the property and Bass Lane running parallel.

Kelsey shook her head. "And the car's still here, so it's not like he left."

Carrie's brow became pointed, her head angled slightly on its axis. "Why would he leave?"

Considering the gap it took for Kelsey to drum up an answer, she got a feeling Carrie didn't wholly buy her response. "Maybe to call and check on the kids. Bad reception out here in the woods."

Carrie suggested, "He could've just gone out for a walk."

Kelsey agreed as much with that more sensible explanation. That had to be it, she thought. Flashes of heat drummed in her face. She felt increasingly silly, embarrassed that her worrying had quickly turned to overreacting. While it didn't feel right that her husband would just go off on his own, exploring the lakeside area on a whim without letting someone know—letting her know—so that they didn't worry about him given he hadn't been feeling well, it wasn't like he had left with the intention of not coming back. Of course he was just out for a walk. The knots in her stomach had wound themselves up for no reason.

Still, Kelsey hoped he was all right. The unknown of his condition nipped at her. Second thoughts had plagued the both of them about coming out here, having to put on the act for their friends that their relationship, their marriage, was rocksteady—the reality being anything but. Denna had been informed when inhibitions were being loosened but had agreed not to let on. Kelsey imagined Ben strolling along the road circling the lake, kicking away at loose stones, lost in how to fake being okay because he didn't want the attention or the pity, living a fib knowing their separation was inching closer. How could he pretend to enjoy himself? How could he put off every thought, every action that could potentially save his marriage when instead he was supposed to be behaving like his marriage didn't need saving? That he wasn't about to crush his children with the news he was going to be staying somewhere else for a while? How did anything else even matter at this point?

Kelsey didn't know the answers. Didn't know how she herself was able to juggle it all. She just wished he was back so she could—

"I'm sure he's fine," Carrie said, returning to the kitchen counter to resume unpacking the different meats for the grill. "He'll be back any minute. Wanna give me a hand?"

"Yeah." To busy her mind elsewhere, Kelsey gathered the blue-and-yellow-checkered vinyl tablecloth along with the packages of napkins and plasticware to help set the picnic table out back. Before stepping out the door, however, she regarded the pair of Ben's glasses she had returned to the worn and pitted top of the coffee table.

Her bad feeling persisted. Those present knots in her stomach intensified.

Even if her husband's headache was gone, or the pain had lessened to where he didn't need to wear them anymore, it wasn't like Ben to leave his glasses just sitting around if he had planned to go off somewhere.

5:18 p.m.

After delivering the plate of dogs and burgers to Pete at the grill, Carrie went back inside and fished the bottle of Midol from her purse, dropping a few pills into her palm and taking them with a full glass of tap water at the sink. She forced herself to chase that down with a second full glass that she drained in one go. She knew better than to start drinking so much with Aunt Flow on her doorstep, not without pregaming with copious amounts of ice water first, but had neglected to do so and was now paying the penalty. Being a little dehydrated always exacerbated her menstrual symptoms.

The headache was precise. An ice pick with a threaded shank lodged in the center of her forehead. The pain wasn't tremendous, but bothersome. Present. A screw being slowly turned. And radiating lightning bolts like the animation of an antenna tower sending out a signal over and over again.

Need to eat, too, she thought. That would help push the headache away. Last thing she had was a dry turkey sandwich and a few red pepper slices at lunchtime with a glass of lightly sweetened iced tea.

She stood at the kitchen sink where a small, propped-open window led out to where her husband was grilling. The charring smell of searing beef mixed with the sprinkling of pepper and onion and garlic salt seasonings that were rubbed into the patties smelled absolutely incredibly divine.

She filled her glass a third time with tap water and drank.

Hopefully, the Midol would kick in before it was time for dinner.

5:22 p.m.

The feat required a few attempts before Teddy could muscle the stakes out of the ground. The eight-inch plastic spikes slid out mostly clean, like a toothpick inserted through the soft crust and then removed to check the status of a baking chocolate cake. What speckles of soil remained on the tapered blades he dusted off with the swipe of a hand before returning them to the gallon ziplock they had been stored in, dropping the bag back inside the musty old box for the badminton set. He had begun separating the sections of poling that made up the net when Denna came out to offer a hand and share some gossip.

"You hear Ben took off?" She kept her voice down as Kelsey was nearby setting the table.

Teddy was also cautious of his volume with their friend in proximity. "What? No. What happened?"

Denna thumbed down the spring bolt holding two of the net rods together and pulled them apart. "Kelsey went in to check on him, and he's gone. But their car's still here."

"So?" The expression on his face changed from mild interest in the developing scandal to mild dissatisfaction as Teddy stood the disassembled rods inside the shabby box. "Doesn't mean he left. Probably just went out for a walk somewhere. Maybe he really loves nature and mosquito bites."

"When you and Ben were going back to the cars, Kelsey told me they've been having problems."

Teddy grimaced with sympathy. He hated to think his friends were going through a rough patch in their marriage and that things remained unresolved while they were all together. "Oh, really? That stinks."

"Ben say anything to you about it?"

He shook his head. They finished taking apart the badminton net and boxing the pieces, careful not to be conspicuous in their whispering while

Kelsey was around. Denna followed her husband inside where he returned the badminton game to the back of the closet.

Teddy said, "You think I should go out and find him? Make sure things are okay?"

Denna chewed on her bottom lip. "Might not be a bad idea? Just to make sure."

"I don't really want to pry," said Teddy. "If there's stuff they're going through, that's really their business. Hopefully they're being honest with each other and can keep it together for everyone's sake." He then gave his wife's arm an innocent jab, displaying squinty eyes and a toothy grin. "That's why we work so well together."

Denna felt she had to reflect that same cheesy smile, though her insides squirmed with turmoil. As per the talk she had with Kelsey earlier, there was a conversation that needed to happen with Teddy about him making a better (i.e., more stable) plan for his future, especially if children were to become an addition to their conjoined life. But timing was everything. Gauging her husband's mood and willingness to listen and be open to change was everything. As a spouse, Denna had learned through trial and error over the years that it wasn't what hard talks to have, it was where and when to have them. Now, amongst their friends for the next twelve hours, wasn't the time, and this solitary lake house wasn't the place.

The back door opened and in came Kelsey with the leftover table settings in hand. Quick on his feet, Teddy improvised a part of some conversation he and Denna weren't having ("And when I saw it, I couldn't believe how big it was!") to dispel suspicion as Kelsey excused herself to pass between them on her way to the kitchen.

"So, I'll just be right back." Teddy gave his wife a quick peck on the cheek before heading out the front door in search of Ben.

Immature, dopey, and aimless as he could be sometimes, Teddy did step up for those around him (though concern for others was never the issue). Denna's critiques of the man were softened, her heart warmed over by the potential in him to not only be the great friend and husband he was on occasion but also a wonderful father.

5:39 p.m.

When a considerable puddle of bubbling juices and blood had pooled on the tops of the eight burger patties, Pete slid the spatula underneath in fluid motions and turned them over. The uncooked sides landed on the hot grates with a loud, spitting *hiss*, the frying grease arousing a geyser of licking flames. He was no grilling expert (what even was "reverse searing" anyway?) but could prepare a delicious burger as long as everyone didn't mind theirs being a skosh beyond crispy (no E. coli was happening on his watch!). The hot dogs he managed on the warming rack, rolling them little by little every minute or so to tan them and keep their grill lines even.

He got the impression something was going on. Denna and Teddy had been murmuring back and forth while taking apart the badminton net. Every so often they'd glanced Kelsey's way as she set the picnic table. Probably wasn't something he wanted to know, and certainly wasn't his business, but curiosity and being on the cusp of whatever whispers and stories were being shared were getting the better of his interest. Had he not been stealing scopes at Denna's shapely legs in her shorts, admiring the fairness of her skin and slopes of her calves, he wouldn't have noticed anything out of the ordinary.

As if daydreaming had the ability to summon, Denna stepped outside carrying a plate with logs of wrapped tinfoil.

"Mind tossing these on?" she asked.

For a second, Pete lost touch with the present when catching the light in her greenish, speckled eyes. "Uh, no problem. What, uh, what are they?"

"I brought some corn on the cob."

It was difficult for him to maintain eye contact. Shifty glances went from her smile, her dimples, the soft curve of her smooth, freckle-dusted neck to the food while it cooked. "Oh. I didn't know you could do corn on the cob on the grill."

"Yeah, it's pretty easy. I just salt and pepper them, put a slice of butter on them, then wrap them up. You cook them for about fifteen…twenty minutes. Just turn them every so often."

"You got it." In the process of accepting the plate, the tips of his fingers ended up overlapping the ends of hers. Denna didn't seem to register this fraction of a moment touch as anything more than incidental whereas Pete's flesh along his arms and shoulders tingled as if his veins were running with Pop Rocks. "Say…uh…" He lowered his voice. "Something…something going on with Kelsey? I just noticed—"

Denna waved this off with a bit of a snicker that showcased cute trenches along the sides of her scrunched nose. "Oh, it's not anything, really, I don't think. Ben's just out for a walk. Kelsey, I think, was concerned because he had a bad headache earlier."

"Oh, yeah, yeah, I know. Well, umm, hopefully…hopefully that's all better, you know?" Busying himself because he couldn't maintain stillness, he shifted the sizzling burger patties over to the left side of the grill and started placing the foil-wrapped corn in rows on the empty, blackened grates. "Can't wait to try one."

Denna smiled. "They're so good."

When she turned and went back inside, the weight of culpability that lay over Pete was as substantial as the connections in his brain firing, the hairs on his arms standing on end the moment his skin had made contact with hers under the plate.

"Stupid," he whispered at himself, closing the lid of the grill with emphasis. "The hell am I doing?"

Staring off at the vast body of the lake through the trees, not seeing the fractals of glinting sunlight coating the water but feeling the oppressiveness of his own indiscretions, Pete internally dragged himself through the muck. He knew he was better than this. Having any sort of feelings for another woman—another married woman at that. It was all harmless, sure. Childish, perhaps. A stupid, indescribable teen-like crush that would go nowhere, absolutely. He would never act upon anything he felt, didn't even wholly understand it. These feelings weren't practical. And given so, why was he having them? Why couldn't he answer that question?

That was what bothered him the most.

"Hey, babe."

Pete startled, not knowing Carrie had come right up next to him.

"Brought you this." She offered an open, sweaty bottle of Sam Adams Cherry Wheat—his favorite brew. "I tried calling to you out the kitchen window, but I don't think you heard me."

Remembering to be aware that Carrie knew nothing of the conflict going on inside his head, he gave his wife a pleasant smile in exchange for the much-appreciated cold drink, a thank-you, then thought better. Thought to reciprocate from the car ride earlier. As she set to go back to the house, he wrapped an arm around her waist and returned her toward him. Before she could question out of surprise, he slid the bridge of his nose alongside hers and laid a gentle but lasting kiss on her. Now that his shirt wasn't wicked with sweat from the badminton game, Carrie wouldn't resist the affection, he knew, and as soon as he felt her lips part, her mouth open, and the warmth of her tongue reach for his, the push and pull of his internal sparring released. Their lips wrapped around, tightening, applying a gentle suction. When they released to the timbre of a soft smack, Pete went wobbly with the slight delirium of oxygen deprivation.

"Wow," Carrie said afterward, nearly breathless. "All that for a beer?"

5:44 p.m.

Teddy hoped he was going the right way. He didn't figure Ben would venture back down Bass Lane in the direction of the main road outside of the woods to call his children without his wife being present, so he made the intuitive decision to continue following the single lane that wrapped around the lake. Given the time of early evening and the thin stack of smoke rising out of the trees to mince with the overcast sky from the back of the lake house where Pete was manning the grill, Teddy was positive Ben would see their food would be ready soon (maybe even smell it in the cooling air) and not stroll the entire loop around the water. Teddy was looking to catch him on the backtrack.

The properties didn't sit right next to each other, but were mostly visible on the cracked and crumbling road from one to the next with a couple football-field lengths of sprouting weeds, low-hanging oak branches, mops of weeping willows, and parched shrubland in between. The small home with the tended yard that Teddy came to at 13 Bass Lane was blue sided with white trim. A two-floor angular Cape Cod that was well-kept with flower boxes under the main floor windows and a built-in, two-story deck on the side that took up as much area as the residence. On a quest to meet up with his friend, Teddy almost bypassed the home entirely until something peculiar deterred his progress.

On approach, there had been the low sound of running and splashing water that Teddy attributed to a fountain feature or some lawn-watering equipment that had to be on the far side, out of sight. As he came around the house, and his view of the other end of the yard opened from the lane, he found that not to be the case.

"Huh."

He was dumbstruck.

A black garden hose with a yellow stripe running like a vein down the line lay snaking along the grass, coming off a looped fixture on the house that kept the long strand from getting tangled. The watering end of the hose wasn't visible. It sat submerged inside of a green plastic wading pool placed out near a clothesline where an exhaustive number of white towels and light laundry hung and rippled and swayed like the nearly two hundred flags at United Nations headquarters. It was evident the hose was still running as the small children's pool was overflowing. The overrun spilled continuously like a mini waterfall over the rim at a dented edge, sloshing and slopping on the oversaturated grass that now lay flat beneath the running excess.

"That's odd."

Teddy wasn't planning on halting his pursuit of Ben, but he didn't feel good bypassing the still-running hose that continued flooding the ground. The homeowner was likely unaware, perhaps forgot it was even running. Maybe they were older and needed help.

Or, he thought, something happened to the kid that the wading pool was being filled for.

Teddy called out, "Hello?"

He stepped onto the fringe of the property to better be heard, cupping a hand around his mouth. "Helloooo? Your…your pool's full!"

No response came from the house. No one came running around from outside to be surprised at the sight of the overspilling pool and to thank him for letting them know so they didn't waste any more water. No one appeared at any of the doors or windows. Teddy next went up to the front door and knocked. Gentle knocking turned to fist pounding and ringing the bell when no one arrived to answer.

"Hello?"

The set of three small windows high on the door were textured on the inside, preventing him from seeing through. There may have been a light on inside the room behind the door, but Teddy couldn't tell. Regardless, no one came in response to his knocking.

As if saying it aloud helped to better justify the weird situation, Teddy said to himself, "Probably left in a hurry and forgot to turn the water off." That seemed enough rationale to wander back around to the side and shut the hose off at the spigot, which he did. The grass in the vicinity had become soupy, his sneakers turned to sponges, soaking up the surplus of water just sitting on top of the ground that could no longer absorb it. He bet some of the groundwater had gotten through the foundation and leaked into the basement.

"Hope they have a sump pump."

He sloshed his way back out to the road, full sneaker prints appearing in his wake when stepping across the concrete drive. At this point, walking had become uncomfortable. His sneakers were waterlogged and heavy. His socks were the same. Each step squelched and squeezed out liquid and small bubbles and dirt. He could feel it oozing between his socked toes. Teddy just wanted to end this nuisance and go back to the lake house.

"Well, Ben, I'm sure you'll be back soon if you're not there already."

With that, he spun with a *squelch* on his wet heels and began a trace of footprints along Bass Lane leading back in the direction of the lake house and the scent and column of grill smoke.

6:03 p.m.

Everyone was spinning their wheels. The burgers and hot dogs were ready and cooling off, everything sitting on plates or in bowls in a make-do row down the middle of the set picnic table. Flies and other curious insects swooped in close to inspect only to be swatted and shooed away while the group remained standing, circled around the table, hovering like the many interested insects, drinks in hand, picking from the chip bowl and veggie and dip appetizers while carrying on short conversations that were but placeholders. Silence fell and side comments were made, then silence reared its head again. Eyes went around, searching for the one brave soul who would make a decision that was anything other than this awkward limbo of waiting.

"Guys, it's okay," Kelsey finally said, relinquishing her will to the situation she couldn't help. "We've waited long enough."

It hurt to suggest moving on without Ben, but she didn't see another choice. She didn't want everyone to suffer with a cold meal or have to discard everything because of the swarming insects notching away here and there at the expense of her husband's unexplained absence. It wasn't fair to all. Ben had been gone almost an hour without notice for reasons only known to him. What initially had raised their concerns at his sudden disappearance was becoming worrisome the longer that disappearance trailed on, evidenced by the uncertain looks she garnered when granting them all permission to sit and eat.

Pete gave the obligatory, "Are you sure?"

She wasn't, but Kelsey did her best to relay comfort with the decision. "Yes."

No one moved. Uncertain eyes still roamed each other's faces. Flies continued zipping in and out.

"Okay, fine, I'll be the first." Foregoing shame and ripping the Band-

Aid off the circumstances, Teddy took the burden upon himself, dipping right in for a seat on the end of the nearest bench at the table. He shoved a handful of Fritos in his mouth in a demonstration that resembled severed tree limbs being fed to a wood chipper while stacking the ingredients for his cheeseburger on both halves of a seeded roll. He didn't lift his eyes to the others to witness their response to his display of brashness, hoping instead that they would be quietly thankful for his icebreaking and follow his lead.

And one at a time they did.

Except Kelsey.

"I'm gonna try calling him," she said. "Maybe there'll be a good enough signal."

There wasn't much confidence in her voice or in her plan, and that frailty earned some lackluster nods while plates were being filled up in the communal disquiet. Citronella candles were lit to repel the tiny pests flying around. Hands reached across the table, crossing in front of one another like some makeshift game of Twister to grab with hands and scoop with spoons and pierce with forks. Low-voiced conversations began keying up once again.

Kelsey's phone was in her purse next to the coffee table. While typing the first letters of his name to bring Ben (listed as Benjamin for the reason that she was just that formal) up in her contacts, she couldn't determine what her response would be if the call went through and he answered. She was angry, confused, worried, and sure, a little scared—how that all would come expelling out of her mouth would be a spur-of-the-moment matter.

She wanted to scream at him but was sure when he answered, her anger would deteriorate into relief.

For what felt like too long, the call timer remained at zero. The outgoing call had yet to go through and ring. Kelsey itched at the sweat pooling on her hairline and the nape of her neck, feeling the tautness of the muscles stretching across her shoulders while walking patterns around the furniture in the living space. "Come on."

Through the open windows, she heard the collective of her friends' voices, not quite what they were saying but that they were talking to each other—everything sounding normal in volume and cadence—and that made this rough instance a little easier to bear. Being out of everyone's sight and beyond the fixture of their immediate attention, she could give in to the panicky feelings and pace, not having to bottle up the anxieties of worrying where her husband had vanished to. Though she was certain they were all talking about her and the missing Ben.

The top left corner of her screen showed her phone had one out of four bars in range of her carrier's LTE network, but the call request wouldn't complete. The connection, spotty as it was, remained out there, reaching, hanging.

"Damn it."

She put the call in the background, opened her text thread with Ben, and quickly typed: Are you ok? Where are you?

She dabbed the arrow to send, and the message entered the thread. A thin green line showing up beneath Ben's contact icon in the header slowly started creeping left to right across the screen, signaling the outgoing text's status in trying to connect with Ben's phone. Wherever it was.

"Come on, come on." Desperate for that little green line to finish the short distance journey to its end point, Kelsey tried to willfully push it along, completing the task.

The green line stretched to the halfway point. Reached three-quarters. Became the width of a fingernail from its end.

There it stopped.

Kelsey grumbled the f-word and ceased her pacing, went to the nearest front window, held her phone up in hopes of topping off with just enough signal to finish the job. A spinning dial icon that looked like a sun showed there was at least minimal network activity. Kelsey pleaded through whispers for the message to send to his phone.

The green line remained millimeters from touching the right end.

Wait, did it just move? Kelsey thought she saw the line inch forward by maybe a pixel or two. Probably not.

She also tried reaching out mentally, a fruitless effort unless somehow Ben was perceptive, sensitive to her worry, could sense her anguish from wherever he had ventured to. Once upon a time it seemed they'd shared that extrasensory connection. When they were younger in love, more attuned to the other's radar, new in parenthood, more optimistic, not as exhausted and rundown and eroded by the demands of their day jobs, the stresses of the pandemic, and the efforts required of them as parents and as a couple at home. As if that little green line on her phone, stuck short of its destination and spinning its wheels, also represented the passage of time, she felt stifled, unable to communicate and locate through the surrounding throng of shadowed woodland.

She whispered into the view out the window that was a summation of endless, towering trees, "Where are you?"

Kelsey startled at the reply.

What came following her question felt cued up, like a band ready to play in front of an eager, passionate crowd where every single person was conjoined in their anticipation and excitement. Cued up and snapping at its apex. A taut guitar string breaking after a simple strum. A piano wire played with a razor blade.

What came following her question took every fear and worry and angst and expounded them by an unknown exponentially. Her heart hiccuped, jolted into a new rhythm.

Caught off guard, Kelsey dropped her phone to the floor—the call still trying to connect, her text still reaching out into the invisible network space to find her husband—and went running out the back door, drawn toward the ensuing commotion where her friends were eating.

What had come following her inquiry, what had jolted her into action, was a blood-chilling scream.

6:08 p.m.

Denna was the one who would claim to have seen it happen. Before that disturbing admission came sputtering out of her mouth like a struggling engine refusing to turn over, she bolted up from the bench, both knees knocking hard against the slatted tabletop, and let loose with a shrill, unabated scream. Her half-full can of hard seltzer rocked on its concave bottom but remained standing while Teddy's long neck of summer ale tipped right over onto its side, making an exclamatory hollow bass note when colliding with the tabletop, rolling and spreading a tide of foamy beer over the spread. In the span of a few risen heartbeats, Pete's and Teddy's faces became stricken and startled as their eyes bounded in every direction from Denna to the table to each other while simultaneous efforts began between them to dam up the spilled beer, find out what had put such a fright into Denna, and express their utter confusion over where Carrie had suddenly gone. She had just been sitting right there.

Kelsey scrambled out the back door. "What's happening?"

"Where'd she go?" Pete shouted to be heard over Denna's hyperventilating cries.

Kelsey was at a loss. "Who?"

Trying to calm his wife, Teddy shook his head at Pete, shouting at him just the same in order to be heard. "I-I don't know."

Kelsey, mystified, spoke mostly to herself. "Carrie?"

Pete called over and over for his wife, who couldn't have gone far but was nowhere in sight.

Trembling and groaning with every exhale, hands pressed into the sides of her face, fingertips clawing from her temples down to her cheeks, bringing red, angry streaks to the surface of her fair skin, Denna gaped in wide-eyed horror, a near-perfect embodiment of Edvard Munch's *The Scream*, at the spot on the bench next to Pete where Carrie had been sitting but was now unoccupied. "She…she…she just…just fucking vanished!"

Except for their hard respirations, Denna's hitching sobs, and the lone chirping of a nearby cricket, an incredulous and bewildered void of silence unspooled, weighing over them, thickening the air.

"What?" Pete recoiled, shaking his head. Denna's claim brought him out of his panicked mindset. He couldn't fathom something so ridiculous. There was no way he heard her correctly. Carrie had been sitting right next to him on the same bench seat not thirty seconds ago. He'd looked right at her and smiled. Patted her left thigh before they started eating. He was taking a swill from his beer when Denna startled everyone by jumping up out of her seat across from them, upsetting the order of the spread on the table by hitting the edge with her knees, and began yelling hysterics. Pete expected Denna to claim a bug was crawling on her, had gotten into her shirt somehow, or something to that effect. Something normal. Not something so out of left field.

Again, Pete shouted for his wife because her disappearance, in the way Denna described it, couldn't have happened. Infeasible. He didn't feel nor hear his wife rise from the bench beside him, but that didn't mean she hadn't. She wasn't at the table and had somehow gone somewhere quickly and without anyone—not including the hysterical Denna—seeing her, but that didn't mean she'd vanished into thin air—that couldn't happen! But what did worry him was that Carrie hadn't yet responded to his calls for her, hadn't reappeared after Denna began shrieking. Pete's panicked voice carried again and echoed across the lake, answered by the despondent cry of a distant loon.

Kelsey was the first to find composure, enough so to ask steadily, "What do you mean she just vanished?"

Denna blinked and blinked as if her eyes had become apertures snapping dozens of pictures for the sake of committing this horrific moment to memory. Or maybe she was trying to erase what she'd seen—replacing those seared images with anything else. Teddy kept telling her in the most soothing voice he could manage that it was okay, it was all okay. Reminding her to just breathe.

"Care?" That was Pete's shorthand for his wife, which came out half as strong, more a desperate plea made in whimper than his previous attempts calling for her. He was fixated on Denna, but for the sole reason of awaiting her explanation at their behest.

Stepping forward, Kelsey entered Denna's line of sight to demand attention and force the latter's cooperation. "Dee." When their eyes met and Kelsey was satisfied, she softened up a bit for the sake of getting a straight answer. "Can you tell us what you saw?"

"It's okay," repeated Teddy, rubbing Denna's arms and giving her hands a squeeze, giving what support he felt he could. As her respirations slowed, became more settled and even though the intakes had remained sharp and fluttering, and the fright in her eyes subdued despite the emergence of tears that were birthed and streaking down the unsettled finger stripes of bloodshot flesh of her cheeks, Denna was able to conjure enough for a few short sentences separated by hitching breaths between.

"She was…she was sitting…right there." Denna resumed fixating on the end of the bench where Carrie had once been but was no more. "I saw her. Then I saw her…just…disappear."

There was no question in her voice. A measure of disbelief existed in the undertone because what she was describing wasn't some common occurrence, but there was a solid, eerie assurance in her truth. Her version of the truth. She clearly didn't want to trust in it, but at the same time she didn't question what had just transpired before her eyes.

"I can still see her face. Right before it happened." Denna swallowed. She closed her eyes, severing a fresh tear to stretch and dribble an inconsistent trail down to her jaw. Her words were direct despite a tremble in her lower lip. "She knew something. Something wasn't right." That strength she mustered to be able to speak and speak clearly deteriorated. Denna sniffled and began to sob. "Then she was just…gone."

No words.

No one dared to move.

No one shared a look.

Except to the empty spot on the bench and the place setting that Carrie had once occupied.

From somewhere across the lake, the loon once again performed in solo, wailing the chorus of its mournful song.

6:10 p.m.

Teddy held his crying wife and wouldn't turn an eye to the others. He didn't want to see the impressions set into their faces. The shock. The fear. He didn't want to see the curled exasperations of how loony they thought his wife had become. Teddy found himself conflicted to defend the bold claim Denna had made, the horrific yet absurd one that, by her fraught reactions, she believed to be true whether or not she was mistaken. Teddy dreaded looking at Kelsey and Pete and seeing in their faces a confirmation of what he knew he would mirror right back to them. Uncertainty. Distrust. The likelihood that Denna had lost her fucking marbles.

Or what if they believed her?

The question though remained unanswered: where did Carrie go?

"Shhh, it's okay." He played this soothing track on repeat until something better presented itself. Teddy mentally cursed himself for not seeing anything.

The scenario replayed in his thoughts.

Kelsey had gone inside to try and call Ben, telling everyone to go ahead and eat. Teddy was the one who'd made the graceless choice to break away from the hesitant group and go first, sitting at the table and filling up his plate to be the voluntary icebreaker. He didn't mind making the move—the persistent hunger cries from his stomach lessened his pride and shame. Eventually, the others were not so evidently ashamed to follow suit. They just needed a leader. Their stilted, rudimentary dialogue about how good the food looked, and how it hopefully tasted as good as it looked and smelled as they also piled it on, quickly detoured to spitballing thoughts about Ben and his whereabouts. The conversation valve loosened, turned, and opened, the lines flowing freely as they engaged in some fresh, juicy gossip.

"Kelsey told me her and Ben have been having problems," said Denna out the side of her mouth that wasn't busy chewing on a forkful of leafy salad.

Carrie asked, "Do you think he really left? I mean, their car is still here. Where would he go?"

"Maybe he planned it so someone would pick him up?" Teddy swallowed and had to repeat this after trying to talk with a mash of cheeseburger clogging up his mouth and wiped a smear of ketchup from his upper lip. At the risk of playing devil's advocate and instigating the conspiratory rumor mill, he tacked on a suggestion. "Maybe there's someone else on the side?"

"Ben's not like that." Cutting in and speaking out in such a stern, direct manner, Pete's stone-cold demeanor and unblinking eyes weren't in line with the airy postulations of the others. "I don't know what's going on with them, but he wouldn't do that. Not to his kids. Not to his wife."

For a beat there was silence. Pete let that quiet continue to speak for him, letting them know a line was being crossed and to tread carefully.

"Kelsey's probably been driving him nuts," Denna interjected. "All she does is work. I'm surprised she didn't bring her work bag with her out here."

Teddy stabbed a cube of watermelon with a plastic fork. "Who's to say she didn't?"

"Hey, you okay?" Pete asked his wife. Attention sidetracked to Carrie, who wore a sober expression of pain with both eyes closed. She pressed the ends of her fingers deep into the center of her forehead, pushing up wrinkles on her brow.

"Yeah. Just a headache. No big deal. I already took something for it."

It seemed not a minute later Denna shot up from her seat and started hollering. Teddy hadn't seen anything other than Carrie was there one second, then he had eyes on the cob of sweetened corn he dusted with a little bit of salt, a little bit of pepper, before grinding and typewriting with his teeth across it. When the scream happened, their group of four at the table had become three.

So where had Carrie gone?

6:10 p.m.

He detested hearing everyone become feckless and get so comfortable speculating and postulating and speaking derogatory hearsay, churning up the muddied waters of other people's business in such dismissive tones that relegated the subjects of the topic into nothing more than collateral damage. The ones they spoke so cavalierly about weren't faceless silhouettes or nameless background casualties like in a war movie; they were their friends. People they had known for years. People they had invited into their homes and considered extended family. The pandemic put some (necessary and understandable) distance between their tribes, but it didn't erase the bonds completely. And when Ben's character started becoming the target of a verbal firing squad, Pete could no longer sit idle and let the others resume their prattling spew.

After he made his point about what kind of man he knew his friend Ben to be and that they were all finding it a little too easy treading these dangerous waters by speaking of someone who wasn't around to defend himself, Pete had looked hard at the other faces at the table, even his wife's.

Rather than continue down the road of tale-telling and presuming about Ben's wandering eye (of which Pete felt a stab of ironic guilt over), the other three moved on to lambaste Kelsey's supposed love affair with her job. Pete could only internally shake his head, curse it all, and continue to eat rather than partake in the gossip train. Not long after, his wife winced in discomfort.

Just a little headache, she'd claimed, and she'd already taken something for it.

That momentary divergence from the scandalous whispers of Ben's and Kelsey's possible indiscretions was enough to drive a stake through the conversation's heart. The two couples at the table went back to picking at their meals while Kelsey remained inside the lake house trying to get ahold of her husband, who'd absconded to God knows where. With the shoddy reception, Pete didn't know if she would get through as he had occasionally glanced at his own phone to check the signal strength (weak then suddenly full bars coming in on a breeze before becoming weak again), planning to call his sister and check on Ava before it got too late, but kept a little optimism that Kelsey would rejoin them with good news.

Carrie gave Pete a nudge with her shoulder, an attempt to reconcile for her part in engaging in such off-putting remarks about their friends. Pete acknowledged her with a pleasant smile that said "all is forgiven, now let's move on" and then he applied a gentle squeeze to her upper leg.

Just as he finished drawing a line of ketchup along the length of his hot dog and going next for the spicy mustard, Denna leapt up from the table and screamed.

His wife was gone. Carrie had been right there next to him, inches from him on the bench. Pete never felt her move or stand. She was just there one moment and then impossibly no longer there the next.

In the commotion he shouted for her only to be ignored. Teddy claimed he didn't see anything happen, but Denna was all about sharing what she saw. Or, what she thought she saw.

The visage of absolute fright consumed Denna's every expression, tears cleaving and falling, while blubbering through catches in her throat an impossible scenario she claimed to have witnessed. The bizarre combination of her stricken look, angry red lines rising on the sides of her face from how she had absently clawed herself in fear, and this unabashed belief in an infeasible scenario manifested a confused terror in Pete.

He called again for his wife, loud as his voice would go without breaking.

This can't be happening.

The same loon from across the lake replied apologetically, but Carrie did not answer him.

This can't be…

Then, his mind entertained the worst.

Could it?

6:10 p.m.

There was no better or more succinct way for Denna to explain what she witnessed. Despite mental pushback of what was plausible, the moment kept revisiting her mind in a disturbing instant replay, each iteration turning fuzzier, but the haunting memory that refused to be cordoned off or go away brought on a palpable dread that caused her stomach to clench and wring, her nose to run, fresh tears to dribble down her face, and an absolute confirmation—despite what the laws of physics might argue—that she was horribly, terrifyingly right, much as she wished she wasn't.

Denna couldn't unsee the look that invaded Carrie's face right before it happened.

That expression of dawning realization in her eyes, in the curvature of her mouth. A surprise. A gasp to likely follow from her parting lips that never came. Maybe a pain or a relief from pain was experienced. Perhaps she even knew what was about to happen.

Denna would never know.

In an instant Carrie faded to nothing. Erased was another way, a much more macabre way, Denna couldn't help but think of it.

Without so much as a sound or a change in the atmosphere, she was there and then undone.

As if she never existed at all.

6:13 p.m.

Kelsey didn't want to believe what Denna was saying because of the dawning implication.

And yet, the tinglings of revelation fired worries throughout her brain. Connections were made. Hairs stood. Goose bumps flared. The puzzle pieces fit together.

The answer to her problem—why her phone, which she realized now was no longer in her hand and must be somewhere on the floor inside, wouldn't connect to Ben—became a whole new reason to be afraid.

If Carrie had indeed vanished into thin air…

Had the same thing happened to her husband?

The frightening answer of her husband's possible fate directed Kelsey into a panicked dash back inside the house. Her phone, having slipped from her grasp at Denna's sudden ear-splitting shriek, lay screen side down on the floor beneath the very window she had been looking out when trying in vain (and against the constraints of human ability) to pray and mentally push the outgoing call to reach Ben's cell. Turning the device over in her hand, Kelsey was unnerved to find the screen lit and the outgoing call still trying to locate her husband's phone. The status beneath Ben's name and number read *Calling…* with the call timer remaining stationary at zero minutes and zero seconds.

"What is it?" Denna had come inside, Teddy and Pete flanking right behind her, the screen door closing. The three wore the pale and wide-eyed disoriented expressions reminiscent of frightened, distressed children looking for someone to comfort them, tell them things were not as bad as they seemed.

Kelsey showed them her phone. "It still can't find him."

Everyone took deep breaths in a collective moment seemingly taken to gain bearings during the developing situation. Pete ran both hands over his bald head, rubbed his eyes with his palms, then opened the screen door and called out for Carrie again. Denna crossed the room, her rubber sandals scuffing on the hardwood floor, and examined Kelsey's phone as if she needed to see for herself the outgoing call had stalled out. No words were exchanged, just an apologetic look from Denna. Beyond that…nothing.

Pete pinched and picked at his bottom lip and the corners of his mouth, looking shaken and lost and not sure. He closed the door. "What…what the hell is going on?"

"Okay," said Teddy, hands up, head bowed to indicate an unconditional surrender. He stepped into the middle of the room, the manner and cadence of his speech reflecting how fed up he had become. "This isn't funny anymore." He broadened his volume to presumably reach the others who were not amongst the four of them populating the living room. "I'll admit it—you got me. You got me good. You guys can come out now."

Everyone searched the small interior of the lake home from where they stood, waiting for something to happen. Nothing did.

When he didn't get what he wanted, Teddy sighed, stalked to the closet door beside where Pete stood, and flung it open. "I said—"

The inside of the closet had a few of the homeowner's jackets hanging on a metal rod, a pair of rubber boots on the floor, a snow shovel, and a few other personal knickknacks along with the boxed-up badminton game set in the back right corner. There was nothing else of interest.

"All right." Teddy tilted his head far to the left then all the way right, producing a short series of pops and cracks in his neck, then went with that same determination to the closed bathroom door. He paused after snatching hold of the knob, gave a gentle courtesy knock, then proceeded to twist the knob and shove the door all the way open. The door banged off the white-tiled wall inside. Like the closet, the bathroom was dim and void of occupants.

Teddy looked up to the ceiling. "Is there a crawl space or an attic in this place?"

Shrugs and glances of confusion made the rounds.

"A crawl space for what?" Kelsey asked.

"For people to hide."

Pete asked, "Who would be hiding?"

Teddy gave him the dead-eyed, mouth agape, "duh" stare. He spoke in slow, thick, singsongy sarcasm. "Uh, Ben and Carrie, obviously."

Soon as he spoke their names, an idea seemed to occur to Teddy, who then charged a tour through the kitchen to the pantry then bolted out the front door on that side of the lake house. The others trailed him. Teddy went to each of their parked vehicles, peeking in the windows, opening the doors to look inside, ending his path at the red panel van parked on the fringe of the property. He climbed into the open back end, rummaged around, then skittered back out.

Denna asked, "What are you doing?"

"They're here, somewhere." Teddy wiped his brow with the inside of his forearm, sweat pooling at his high and thinning hairline. He clasped both hands to his hips, annoyance scribbled on his face. The evening light around them had begun to wane, shadows lengthening in the cover of the towering trees. The magic hour gloam of soft light and murky shadow had descended over the lake. A quiet, high breeze rattled only the leaves and thinnest branches at the tops still saturated in warm, lowering sun. Distant owls hooted, but only a few. Teddy observed the area with a hint of distaste. "Hiding or something. Some game they're playing."

"What *game*?" said Kelsey, to which Pete tagged on there was no game taking place.

"Oh, I see now," said Teddy. He nodded his head, licking his lips. "So this is something you're all in on together. Against me, huh?"

Denna was adamant against this paranoia. "Teddy, I saw what happened. I saw Carrie disappear! And if we don't get out of here, the same thing might happen to all of us. Maybe it's what happened to Ben…"

"Do you hear how ridiculous you sound?" The tail end of *sound* cracked and reverberated, carrying Teddy's agitated and breaking voice outward in an expanding wave, startling a few jittery birds into flight, hitting off the dense tree trunks and sailing across the vast bed of darkening water. "Do you have any idea how *fucking crazy* that is? People don't just vanish into thin air like that."

Pete meekly raised his hand. "There is such a thing as spontaneous combustion."

"This is a *prank*!" exclaimed Teddy. "Plain and simple. I don't know what I did to all of you to make you guys so pissy, but well done. You got me for a minute." He directed a slow golf clap all around.

"Babe..." Denna, visibly fighting to maintain composure, sporting cried-out eyes that were red with flushed cheeks to complement, took a gentle hold of her husband's hands to cease his sarcastic, insensitive applause and hold his attention. "No one's doing anything to you. Something..." She broke her stare to look upward and blink away the emergence of new tears. "Something is very wrong out here."

Teddy yanked his hands from her loving, pleading hold. "You can stop right there. I'm not buying it. The whole disappearing thing—*fake news*. That's what that is. No one just vanishes like that. Doesn't happen." Grinding his teeth, he stiffly dabbed the end of his pointer finger against the center of Denna's forehead. "You can get that insane thought right out of your fucking head right the fuck now."

"Whoa, whoa, all right, all right." Pete stepped in closer to Teddy and Denna to de-escalate. The open palms he held out as a gesture of keeping the peace trembled with his own fright. "Let's just calm down here, okay?"

"Whatever happened, happened right in front of you," Kelsey said to Teddy, her tone on the brink of admonishment, "and you're just going to choose not to believe it?"

Teddy cocked his head at a hard angle with one eye squinted. "Feels like you're trying to say something here, Kelsey."

"Carrie disappeared from the table where you all sat. Denna is the only one who saw it, and you don't believe her? Your own wife?"

"That's right. I don't believe it. I don't believe a *human being* can just disappear into thin air, no matter what she *thinks* she saw." As he spoke now in elevated volume, Teddy pointed right at Kelsey. "Why are *you* making that out to be something I should just accept as fact when it sounds so incredibly stupid, not to mention im-*fucking*-possible?"

Denna's hands flopped to her sides in an act of exhausted acceptance. She sighed. "Because...it happened."

Teddy grunted, rubbing a hand up and down the moist nape of his sweating neck, pacing around in tight lines through the shin-high grass. He approached the push mower that was left as a lawn ornament after cutting only a few yards' worth of grass and gave it a kick. Pete kept his distance as tempers seemed to diminish to a simmer, settling himself against the side of the parked van. He remained stationed between Teddy and the two women. Denna said something no one could hear.

Teddy ceased his pacing. "What was that?"

Denna repeated after clearing her throat, freeing a clogged-up voice. "I said it all makes sense now."

Kelsey asked, "What do you mean? What does?"

Under his breath but loud enough to be heard, Teddy muttered, "None of this makes any fucking sense."

"The downed tree," Denna offered.

Pete stood up straight, stepping away from the side of the deserted van. He folded his arms, skeptical but also intrigued. "What about it?"

"Why hadn't anyone come across it before us? Why had it been there on the road for so long?"

"Here it comes," Teddy mumbled, as if he foresaw the conclusion.

"Maybe because…" Denna swallowed, conjuring the fortitude to say what even she couldn't fathom was about to come out of her mouth. "Because there's no one here anymore."

Teddy responded to this by sighing the Lord's full name in vain and pacing with both hands interlaced behind his head.

Now it was Kelsey speaking up. "You're saying everyone *here*"—she threw her hands out to her sides, signifying their entire surrounding environment—"has disappeared? Like how you're saying Carrie did?"

Hearing it back gave Denna pause as she reconsidered, because in no way did that sound pragmatic. Sounded more like science fiction, to be honest, but she eventually succumbed to acquiescence.

"You know what that sounds like." Pete didn't phrase a question, instead putting out there the obvious takeaway to such a fantastical theory.

Again, Denna nodded. More certain this time. "I know. I know. It sounds…it sounds—"

"Crazy," Teddy interjected, also not intonated in the form of a question. "Nuts. Insane. Un-goddamn-balanced."

Denna set him in her sights with a measure of ferocity, approaching her husband with determination. "You told us what happened when you went looking for Ben. The house next door? The running hose flooding a pool? You said you knocked on the door and called out. No one was around." She motioned at the push mower being Exhibit A. "John. He wouldn't leave his van open and his stuff out like this."

Denna then looked at Kelsey. "Ben…he wouldn't just wander off without telling anyone and then not come back." Then, to Pete. Looking at him broke Denna's heart all over again, her posture and voice began to crumble. "Carrie…"

Denna didn't feel she had to describe for the dozenth time what she saw happen to Carrie.

"Yes, it's crazy. It doesn't make any sort of sense, and I can't explain it. But that doesn't mean it's not what's happening." Denna summed up her resolve to be able to say, without a shred of doubt or tremble in her voice, "For some reason, people here are disappearing."

Quiet glances around revealed the tell in everyone's faces. Nothing between them was obscured, discreet, or ambiguous. They were all poker players holding shitty hands.

Pete was at odds, jumbling so much in his head. Unsure what to believe, but much as he might've wanted to, he couldn't deny or argue the theory based on the presented proof. He might have been pondering up a list of alternatives to debate, but he otherwise looked baffled in the form of asking himself "how can this be?" At the same time, he was coming to terms with the disappearance of his wife, whatever the cause—so much information compounding in his head.

Kelsey was outwardly nervous, biting her lip, shifting weight from foot to foot, restless hands, trying to keep it together while on the cusp of dropping to the ground and imploding into a mess of shrieks and whimpers. She trusted what Denna had said and was struggling to manage.

Then there was Teddy, who thought it was all bullshit.

The croaking of a nearby toad shrouded in the tall grass reminded Denna how she hadn't heard from the faraway loon in a while. Even the owl perched somewhere out in a distant tree had gone quiet. The birds, too. A matter of awareness in the moment, there weren't many chirps or calls or beating wings or any other involuntary sounds from the woodland creatures and water-bound animals as the blanket of dusk settled around them.

The stretch of uneasy quiet within their group was finally snapped by Kelsey who asked what they should do.

This question was directed at Denna, who, by the rapt gazes of the others—including Teddy—granting her their full attention, had become adopted as a sort of de facto decision maker.

"We leave," she said. It was the only answer that felt right. "We go. Right now. Before it happens to us."

There were sighs, groans, and all the other physical stresses of exasperation and being overwhelmed under the circumstances presenting amongst the others. Pacing through the front yard, heads shaking, palms and fingers scrunching brows, muttering under breaths.

"That's easy for you to say," Pete pointed out as if her decision was trivial, indicating Teddy. "You wouldn't be leaving anyone behind."

Denna countered, "It isn't easy. And…we're not leaving the others. They're…just not here anymore."

"Ben is not dead!" The very air shook from Kelsey's thundering declaration, her glassy-eyed determination for that desire to be the truth. The crack produced from her emotionally swollen throat that originated from the very depths of her turmoiled being was hard on the ears and stomach and powerful enough to sound agonizing. Rich enough to spread invisible waves carrying her words to echo outward across the blackening lake. She wiped her eyes, her nose, and softened her words if only to save what remained of her voice to not exhaust herself further. "He's just…missing…somewhere."

"We can't leave." Pete positioned himself closer to Kelsey in the yard, creating the image of a united front. "What if you're wrong? What if you're wrong and they come back?"

Denna wanted to hope for that to be the case. But hope was flimsy. Unreliable. She wished to be more optimistic. She wanted to believe, if nothing else, whatever mysterious source she hypothesized had abducted Ben and Carrie would simply return them, unharmed, maybe unaware of the knowledge (the lone exception being the passage of time) that anything had even happened to them. And along with their return would come the others who had been taken, like John. But that was placing trust in something she knew nothing of, something beyond the natural, something she hadn't witnessed for herself and could only speculate about. That meant lending and encouraging a weak devotion she didn't feel an intrinsic inclination toward. In fact, she suspected the worst. There was a great and potential risk in staying put—a likelihood they would share the same bizarre fate as the others.

She argued back, "What if I'm right? What if they don't come back? What if it happens again to one of us? We have no reason right now to believe it won't."

She then added, to stimulate confidence in her perspective, "What about your kids back home? What about them if something happened to either one or both of you out here?"

Pete and Kelsey looked at one another, possibly in hopes that the other one was sturdier in a decision. The wariness over sacrificing their chance of seeing their children again was on full display. They were mirrors in a silent search for answers, looking for strength and resolve. Neither would answer that they wanted their children raised by anyone other than themselves and their respective spouses, but that firm position wasn't made vocal, only inherent. They were looking to each other, both now considered single parents for an unknown duration, to make a right decision when one wasn't crystal clear to either.

"Okay, okay, I've had enough." Inserting into the absolute center of the conversation, Teddy left the sidelines near the red panel van where he was treading tracks through the high grass to make himself the focal point. His once displeased attitude was now one of a strained, exhausted but not entirely depleted, compassion. "Look, seriously, I love you guys. Really. I do. Even though you're all driving me nuts and it doesn't seem like it right now, I do."

He folded his hands in front of himself, turning to each individual to make a pointed but blanket appeal. "I am begging you—all of you—to listen to yourselves. Listen to what you are saying.

"Now, I'll be honest, I thought what was happening at first was a joke…a terrible joke, yeah. But I think I see now what's really going on. And I think it's a whole lot of denial."

The crossed look that overtook Kelsey's face resembled catching a whiff of fresh roadkill. "Denial about what?"

Teddy absently swatted at a mosquito nearing his left ear, resuming undeterred. "Kelsey…I know you shared some stuff in confidence with Denna earlier. About your marriage. By the look on your face right now, I'm betting you didn't think we would all find out about it. We did. She told us after Ben…well, you know."

Kelsey's mouth repositioned in ways that suggested she was biting her inner cheek, maybe even her tongue to staunch the eruption of words and hurt that burned like stomach acid rising into her throat. Denna made a quiet apology, but Kelsey paid her no mind. "And what's your point?"

Trying to remain sensitive to the situation and also be compassionate, Teddy made a slow, cautious approach toward her. He progressed toward Kelsey's space with a slightly hunched-to-the-side posture, careful to be affable, conscious to remain outside her invisible bubble, although taking himself right to the very edge of that comfort zone. "I think what happened here isn't that Ben went missing, but that he left. Maybe he called someone for a ride or had it set up before we all got here. Whatever arrangement he made, I think you really need to consider the possibility—a possibility far more likely and realistic—that instead of just vanishing into the air like Houdini, he planned to leave all along." Teddy dropped his arms, which had previously been moving and gesticulating with his hands as he spoke, to his sides. "And he did."

The hard shift in her throat spoke to the seed of doubt sprouting roots within Kelsey Renmore. The obvious desire she had held on to for wanting her husband to be all right worked her over as she seemed to withdraw inward, ruminating, journeying inside herself to search for the difficult truth that resided in her molten, unsettled gut and in her galloping heartbeat. She and Ben were planning on a separation as soon as the lake house trip was over. That wasn't a secret in their floundering marriage. Instead, that agreement was meant to be a potential remedy for their personal issues with each other and how they saw the remainder of their marriage playing out, especially in front of Margaret and the twins. What she and Ben would do in the short term was meant to be better for them in the long term. What Teddy was saying made sense, much as she didn't want to believe her husband had left her. But then not wanting to hear it didn't make it untrue. This supposed plan of Ben's secret departure versus the unlikely and highly implausible idea he'd vanished from existence made Teddy's proposed possibility into a more feasible plot.

Maybe he really had taken off.

Pete set his jaw, unfolding his arms, open to the challenge. "And Carrie? What about her? She wasn't upset. She was sitting right there with us and then just…gone. Why would she leave? *How* could she have left, if what Denna said isn't true?"

Teddy set his next course, narrowing his eyes. "Are you so sure she wasn't mad at you?"

"You seem to have it all figured out, so you tell me—what reason would she have to sneak out of here like you say Ben did?"

"I think you know…" Teddy grimaced with sympathy, holding back on a hand he didn't seem interested in playing just yet. "But probably not something you want aired out here in public."

"Try me." Pete didn't so much as flinch. His eyes widened, accepting the dare. "You seem to think we're all overreacting. If you've got all the answers, might as well spill 'em."

Following a moment's pause, fist pressed to mouth where consideration and vigilance appeared to be contemplated, Teddy drew a deep inhale and shrugged, ultimately deciding to hell with it and threw open the gates. "All right, fine, if we're just going to play it like that. You say Carrie couldn't be mad at you and decide to take off from the table, right? Well, here's what I'm thinking—you ready?"

Pete's face remained fixed. Only his eyebrows performed a subtle rise to show he was waiting.

"I think Carrie got pissed because she caught you ogling my wife."

The prepared fixture of stone that had been Pete's default expression throughout the majority of this time slightly altered. His cheeks flexed and shifted, jaw tightened. His eyes broke contact for a fraction of a second. At the same time, Denna blinked, dazed and numb and speechless, thankful that no attention had spun back around to her.

Curious, Teddy squinted one eye at Pete, angling his head to the side. "Oh, what? You…you thought I didn't know? You thought those little glances you stole at my wife…you thought nobody saw them?"

A tide of heat broke its way up Pete's back and neck. Hard as he tried to play it cool and not react, the emittance blushed his skin. In the fading twilight he prayed his guilt wasn't perceptible. Though how he spoke nothing to the contrary was a full admission. Thing was he couldn't yet speak at all, for fear of his throat betraying him, his voice cracking, his tendency to ramble when attempting to lie, or a complete blowing of his top. Responding was too much of a gamble.

When within arm's reach, Teddy, smiling a rather devious smile if such a one were being inspected by a keen eye, reached out and playfully—but creeping on the edge of playfulness—slapped Pete on the arm. "No worries, man. I'm not upset with you. Fact is, I actually take it as a compliment, believe it or not. It's like you're telling me I've got good taste."

It was then Teddy attended to his wife with a smile that may also have held a hint of mischievousness. "And I do."

Denna could only shake her head, put off by this grotesque and boastful display by her husband. "You're an asshole." At times like this, when he committed himself to full-on douchery, she was thankful they didn't share a child.

"That may be," Teddy agreed, hitting each word with a lyrical emphasis, and now he was really off to the races playing into the act. Being full of himself and brash. His movements took on a certain fluidity, a jester's dance as he wove his way around the three stationed in the yard's gloom who either sneered at him or expressed a restrained repulsion at his delight. That repulsion, he thought, could have also been self-directed as he pointed out the faults they tried so hard to keep hidden.

"But sometimes, my loving—and *lovely* (he said this while making eyes at Pete)—wife, an asshole is what everyone needs. It's what they need to wake them up to what's really going on."

"This is getting fucking old," said Kelsey. "Instead of *this*, can't we be doing something constructive? We need to figure out what's going on. We need to find Ben and Carrie."

"And you can have right at that, sister," chimed Teddy with a snap of his fingers. "But you'll be doing it sans two because we're done here."

His voice then heightened into announcement mode as he began cutting a swath across the unkempt yard toward his and Denna's vehicle parked on the far end, his message going out to the dark and motionless lake, to the tiny bloodsuckers whizzing by his face, to all the darkening trees standing in audience around them, and to the unseen creatures nestling in for the night.

"Thank you all for a spectacular evening! Sorry to cut it short, but I'll take my company with a whole lot less crazy-ass insanity."

Teddy almost made it to the Wrangler before realizing he wasn't being accompanied. "Let's go."

Denna remained grounded. "We can't just leave them."

"You're the one who said we had to leave!"

"Together," said Denna, calm and steady as the quiet lake water. A large tear ran a fast trail down her face, defying her rocksteady stance. "We can't go without them."

"They don't want to leave!" Teddy tugged at the side remnants of receding hair still on his head.

"The headaches."

Everyone turned to Kelsey, who spoke up. A dawning brightened her face from the previous disgust toward Teddy that had hardened her.

"Ben said he got a headache right as we got here."

Pete was struck with a similar epiphany. "Carrie had a headache at dinner."

"So what?" said Teddy. "Like that means something?"

"It's a commonality, you idiot." Denna felt a stab of shame for name-calling her husband, especially in front of others, but his flat-out denial and questioning of what was beginning to make sense of this craziness was annoying as shit. She closed her eyes, shook her head, sending feelers to perform an internal systems check. "I feel fine."

Pete did a similar status check. "Me too."

"I had the beginnings of a headache when we got here," said Kelsey, "but I figured it was allergies. It went away a while ago."

"Excuse me!" shouted Teddy, as obnoxious as can be. If any nearby animals in the woods had slumbered their way into their holes, ready for bed, they were certainly popping bloodshot eyes open in annoyance. Teddy stepped around the front of his Jeep. "What are you all getting at?"

Denna, Kelsey, and Pete looked to one another, finding in each other's inspired faces a compatible, unspoken agreement.

A relieved half smile curled Pete's lip. "As long as we don't have the headache, we should be all right."

Before her husband could raise a dispute, Denna reached out, hoping to summon and bring out of him what sympathy, sensitivity, and humanity she knew he had in spades, when he wanted to have them and showcase them.

"Stay. Please. Help us find the others if they can be found. Help us figure things out if we can. The moment one of us feels a headache coming on, we'll leave." She went to the others for confirmation and their allegiance to this plan. "All of us."

Pete and Kelsey gave their mutual pledge. "All of us."

Denna added, "We have to warn others about whatever's happening here."

For a sound and considerable amount of time, Teddy considered the proposed agenda, nodding his head along. But when his smile broke, and the whites of his teeth could be seen in the dim, Denna knew she had lost him.

"No thanks," he said, trying not to burst at the seams with laughter. "I'll be checking out of this funny farm. You all can stand in a circle and activate your 'wonder powers' like a bunch of jackasses, but not me." He sauntered back around to the driver's side, popping open the door. He then said to Denna, "If you're not coming with me, maybe one of them will give you a ride home. I'm sure Pete won't let you down."

Letting that disdainful salvo be his parting shot, Teddy started up the Jeep, flipped the headlights on, backed out onto Bass Lane, and gave a double-shot honk of the horn and a giddy wave out the downed window as he drove off in the direction of the main road.

She wasn't certain because of her failing vision in the diminishing daylight, the sun now behind the tops of the trees, but Kelsey swore that departing wave of Teddy's went from displaying all five fingers to just one.

6:38 p.m.

"I'm sorry," said Pete. The magnitude of everything he was apologizing for but couldn't articulate into better words rested in the weight of that inadequate, sweeping acknowledgment, hoping to be allowed off the hook for his sins.

"It's fine." Denna watched the two red taillights of the Jeep Wrangler shrink away until the growing distance and collective of trees in the twilight made them no longer visible. "He'll drive around for a bit then feel really terrible and come back. It's just…how he handles things sometimes when he's overwhelmed." She hated defending her husband's overreaction to their dire predicament, hoping for his return to at least redeem himself. Teddy could be a great guy, but also had a very Dr. Jekyll/Mr. Hyde-type personality that reared its head every so often. His behavior of storming off wasn't conducive to their current situation, but options and alternatives weren't available. He'd come around on his own time and when he was ready, even if the timing wasn't beneficial. So being he couldn't be counted on, Denna pivoted away from her husband, not wishing to dwell on him and the things she had no control over when, in their immediacy, they faced more grim circumstances. "So, what do we do?"

"What *can* we do?" Pete asked. Kelsey joined them at the panel van. From his back pocket he pulled out his phone to check the home screen for the time—twenty minutes to seven. He also noted his battery was down to 42 percent, a result of the device constantly searching for a connection. "It'll be dark soon."

A little less than three weeks before the autumnal equinox, the late summer sun was closing in on the distant black hills of the western horizon, but like a major city forested with skyscrapers, the floor of the woods at Echo Lake would exist in obstructed dark long before the outside world of upstate New York at this time with its scenic, warm-lit hills and shadowed valleys.

"Maybe I'll take a drive around the lake, see if I can see anything." Pete didn't know how best to pass the time when there wasn't a clear direction on what to do, or where to look for Ben or Carrie, if they could be found at all. Waiting around for something to happen felt futile and insufficient when his wife and friend were missing. There was also no telling where they were in their race against the clock—how long before one of them staying at the lake became symptomatic with the headache that they deduced to be the only forewarning. "I can't just sit here—it doesn't feel right. Not if Carrie and Ben are out there somewhere. I won't take long."

"I'll stay in case they show back up." Kelsey didn't seem thrilled to take up that particular mantle either, but she added, "Someone has to be here."

Denna took a moment, deciding. "If it's all right, I'll tag along with you?"

Pete nodded. "Sure. Everyone's still feeling fine?"

Kelsey said with a shrug and a sigh, "Yeah. I guess. Given the situation…"

Without going into further detail, they all shared agreement that they were doing the best they could despite the unknowns of what they were up against.

"Okay." Pete took out his key fob and pressed to unlock the doors. A chirp from the vehicle accompanied the release of the door locks. The blinking headlights on his Mazda 6 strobed quick flashes of white light over the front of the house and the yard. "We'll be right back."

Denna gave a shallow, solemn wave to her friend staying behind.

"See you in a few minutes," said Kelsey.

Pete echoed with determined reassurance, "A few minutes."

The foreboding uneasiness made that promise feel like a lie.

6:44 p.m.

"Stupid morons."

Being the lone occupant of the Jeep Wrangler coasting along the high-beamed stretch of Bass Lane, bouncing around hard in the seat as the tires rolled over the uneven pavement pockmarked with spiderwebbed cracks and nasty divots, Teddy let fly with every frustration.

He mimicked Pete in whiny, nasally tones. "As long as we don't have the headache, we should be all right." Then he cut loose with a raging howl of colorful language before lowering the visor above his head and smacking it back into place. He punched the dashboard, slapped the steering wheel silly as one of the Three Stooges would when punishing each other, pounded on the horn, and made faces at himself in the rearview before knocking the mirror askew with his fist. None of this outburst was cathartic, only more enraging. He could feel his blood bubbling, boiling over. Even with the windows down and the chilly rush of evening air from the woods coming in, his body temperature had an adverse response—rising to where he broke a sweat doing all his venting.

"We can't just leave them."

That mimicry was of his wife being the group's mental compass, to which he answered himself.

"Uh, sure can!"

His voice started to wear thin and raspy from the heavy shouting.

"Sure did just leave them."

That muttering admission wrenched at his insides. An unpleasant emptiness growled, tunneling through his stomach.

Nothing ahead of him but the long, lone, broken stretch of Bass Lane and flanking trees, branches reaching out along the shoulder like fans at a sporting event trying to nab a touch of their favorite players running by.

Teddy resumed popping away with jabs and pounding fists on the dash and wheel and visor and mirror. He cursed himself for leaving Denna back there. He should have made her come with him—what the hell was he thinking just leaving her?

He sighed. The anger that swelled his chest deflated. He couldn't go back. Not yet. It hadn't nearly been long enough. There was no way to fend off (much-deserved) criticism or save any kind of face after behaving and storming off as he did. And, he considered (now regretfully), firing off the middle finger while peeling away may not help his case when he went back. What could he say? He had been reactionary instead of sound minded.

"Stressful times," he said to himself, trying to justify how he had acted. He fixed the rearview mirror—relieved the neck didn't snap and the rounded rectangle of framed reflective glass didn't drop off into his hand when he twisted it back around and into position—so that he could see himself. "They'll understand. I didn't mean anything by it."

His wind-whipped face burned warm knowing that was false.

Teddy verbalized his pent-up resentments with a long groan. He'd gotten himself so worked up, so angry, his blood pressure spiking out of nowhere, that the quick drain off left his head woozy with a tenacious pulsing behind his eyes. Night driving and having to strain to see sharply even with the assistance of the high beams wasn't making anything better.

"Note to self: I need to get my eyes checked."

Off the sides of the road ahead, quickly approaching, in the peripherals of the high-beam headlights, lay the sawed-off lengths of the fallen ash tree. In passing those amputated segments, Teddy thought of Ben, and a stab of sorrow sobered him up to the reality that he may not have agreed with the others in the matter regarding the case of his friend's vanishing but that he also wasn't contributing to the efforts to help find him. His wife and Pete and Kelsey had stayed behind to figure out where Ben and Carrie had gone because they were worried. Teddy, meanwhile, was sulking due to his selfishness and lashing out.

Teddy grunted frustration at himself, knowing he was wrong, knowing he wasn't being helpful, and ready to admit it beyond just to the audience of himself.

Before he could reason that it was the right time to slow down and perform a K-turn, the pressure in his head amplified. The amount of pain tripled quickly enough that his vision blurred, his ears rang with hollow bells, then that pain spiked some more. Teddy took one hand off the wheel and gouged fingers into the pressure points across his brow, hoping to stave off some of the squeezing, sirening agony. None of it helped. It got so bad his sole focus became hissing and groaning and squinting to see anything through the out-of-focus hazes of white light cast by the headlamps of his Jeep.

Sick to his stomach from the searing torment of screaming hellfire in his head with a multitude of color bursts exploding across his field of vision, Teddy could only cry out a long, garbled, doleful moan as his brain began browning out. He retained enough awareness to slip his foot off the gas, though a heavy right hand clutched to the steering wheel veered the Jeep off the loosened gravel road. The deep grooves in the Jeep's tires kicked up displaced chunks of asphalt and stones on the shoulder then loosened earth in their wake as the vehicle tread and carved a winding path off-road.

Before the invisible vice crushing his head accomplished the feat of surrendering him into unconsciousness, the front of the Jeep accordioned into a mass of scaling tree trunks that only tremored and remained upright as Teddy was pitched into the windshield having neglected to buckle up.

A sticky, syrupy warmth ran over the dips and curves of his face, spreading over his closed eyes. When the oozing reached his upper lip, he managed to peek his tongue out just enough to flavor the strong coppery taste of his own blood that reminded him of sticking coins in his mouth as a very young child. Teddy attempted to pick up his head, but his neck wouldn't have it. He felt nothing but wave after wave of incessantly scalding throbs without being able to place the source. The only comfort was in not moving. Unable to reorientate and account for the wherewithal of each limb and each appendage, he gave into the enveloping world that was turning black and soundless and, eventually, painless.

6:47 p.m.

Pete kept mentally thanking God that the inside of the Mazda's cabin was dim. *Not that God had anything to really do with it*, he thought, but more so the timing of the day with the sky reaching into the orange-and-purple shades of dusk and inkier hues at ground level. Although the sentiment was all the same, he supposed, if God indeed created the heavens and the earth—he had *something* to do with the cycle of daylight and hours of darkness and their transitions in between, so Pete's gratefulness, he guessed, wasn't totally misplaced. He also realized he was doing anything and everything to avoid looking at or thinking about the woman in the passenger seat a foot and a half to his right.

The left side of his face—the far side turned away from Denna—kept contorting and flexing and grimacing and expressing all of his discomforts. The right side that was open to her he kept as still and as expressionless as possible. Although they were obscured in the dark, minus those pesky little dashboard lights that illuminated all the gadget buttons and the readable outputs for his speed and gas level and how cool/hot the engine was, he wasn't about to pick his nose thinking she couldn't see him if her night vision was adequate. He also didn't dare risk turning his head for fear of spotting the enormous elephant sitting between them. The unspoken question gnawing at him, eroding his restraint, was how long could they ignore it?

Pete determined not long once he opened his mouth instead of thinking first.

"Hey, uh, I just want to say, about what Teddy said earli—"

"It's fine."

The deepening shadows and the drapes of her chin-length auburn hair kept most of Denna's face out of view. When he shifted his eyes over, she was angled toward the passenger window, expression impossible to determine.

Judging by the sound of her voice, he heard an unmistakable "not right now" sentiment. Understandable. This was obviously a subject she wanted to continue to avoid for any plethora and combination of reasons. Pete didn't blame her.

"Hey," said Denna, chippering up, "you see that?"

What she pointed at, tapping on the glass, out the passenger side window wasn't hard to spot coming around a cluster of trees in the inky, oppressive blues preceding absolute dark. A square of light. Light from inside a window. A window that was set near a side door of a small Cape Cod that led out to the upper level of a large, two-floor deck.

Pete drove up onto the lawn, never minding having to mount the sharp bump of the incline going off Bass Lane and apologized for the instant decision. He hastily parked (almost neglecting to put the transmission into Park before turning off the engine), and as they got out he noticed a glimmering of water in a wading pool sitting next to the far side of the house. The clear surface mirrored the last fractals of light in the changing sky.

"This is the house Teddy was at." Pete remembered hearing about the pool, which now wasn't overflowing. The seven inches or so of water inside the plastic tub had settled. A crack in the plastic lip of the rim remained puckered outward.

Denna raced up the deck stairs with Pete right behind her. She knocked, calling out hello, peeking inside, trying to see between the drawn blinds spaced barely an inch open. The interior light they saw was coming from a ceiling fixture in the dining room, which sat beyond a darkened kitchen inside the door.

She knocked again, louder this time. "Hello?"

Pete could only imagine the lack of any answer was making Denna just as impatient as it was him. "Is the door unlocked?"

In another time, under a different set of circumstances, the thought of committing a misdemeanor with little conscience wouldn't have occurred to Denna. She would never proclaim herself a Girl Scout over the period of her four decades plus (her mid-to-late twenties were a minefield of questionable choices and exes), but gladly partaking in illegal trespassing wasn't a notable item to be checked off on her bucket list. In this time, however, growing more dire and unpredictable and unexpected as the seconds ticked by, there wasn't much in the way of hesitancy. Rather than express uncertainty to Pete, she turned the silver lever on the door herself and gave a push.

The door swept easily open.

"Hello?" Denna leaned in over the threshold, keeping her feet planted on the straw welcome mat on the deck, not yet committing to following through with the act of intrusion. "Anyone home?"

Pete leaned in over her, shouting, "Police department. Just checking to see if everyone's all right."

"What are you doing?" Denna whispered. "It's a crime to say you're a cop."

"Is it any less of a crime than entering someone's house?"

Denna sighed. "That's fair."

Still, no one from inside responded.

They crossed the white metal transition strip acting as the barrier separating outside and inside, stepping onto the white hexagonal-tiled floor of the kitchen. No turning back. Nothing seemed unusual or out of place until Pete indicated a pan sitting on a front burner on the stove, illuminated in the pale light coming in through the windows over the deep double sink. The shallow pan had what they determined to be caked-on egg residue, yellowish brown and flaky.

Denna used the slotted flipper resting on the counter next to the stove, trying to scrape the remnants off the pan, but to no avail. "It's been here a while." Next, they entered the lit dining room, walking around opposite sides of the dressed table where green porcelain plates, silver utensils, two tall glasses, and two small plastic cups (one with the cast from *PAW Patrol* and one with Barbie) were set in front of each of the four chairs, slightly pushed back. The table settings were by no means spotless. Piles of half-eaten, hardened scrambled eggs, gnawed on triangles and rectangles of stale toast, full and bitten links of sausage, and withered hunks of various berries were left to neglect on the plates. Congealed orange juice remained in the tall glasses, pulp staining the insides, while the children's cups contained old and stinking milk.

"It's like they just vanished," said Denna. "Right in the middle of eating."

Pete took up one of the kids' cups and sniffed. Not that he thought the spoiled milk wasn't real—he knew, though acceptance was an admittance of its own kind—but he prayed against all the visible, obvious proof to be wrong. Because it had to be wrong. People didn't just literally disappear without a trace. At the recoil from the wretched milk, something else sour occurred to him. "There are no flies."

Indeed, not one gnat, not one housefly or fruit fly occupied the table or flew circles in the air around the dining room—nothing taking advantage of the naked, unprotected scraps left out to rot.

The unusual setting laid out before them in the dining room turned more macabre.

"Did you learn about Roanoke when you were in school?" Pete asked, to which Denna only met his eyes. "A whole colony of people just vanished. But what was weird were the rumors that tables still had food on them, as if the people just got up and left in the middle of a meal. Didn't even bother to finish. Like something took them. None of the colonists were ever found, not one trace."

Denna absorbed their surroundings again, seeing it all through a different lens now. The skittery feeling of impending doom, of goose bumps poking out of her skin, and the chill of ice water in her veins bringing her to shiver. Surrendering to an awful intuition that turned her stomach, that maybe there wasn't anything to discover—no answers, no clues to the whereabouts of the missing Ben and Carrie or John or anyone else at Echo Lake, as surely every one of the other houses closely resembled this one. That soon enough, she and Pete and Kelsey would succumb to the same fate that had no name and wore no face. Only a matter of time. "Maybe we do need to leave. While we can."

Pete wasn't about to argue. "Let's get Kelsey and get the hell outta here."

7:02 p.m.

Stepping on the pedal to fling open the trash can lid, Kelsey upended the large plastic bowl, gravity pulling the half dozen or so salad ingredients tumbling into the waste bag, leaving a sliver or two of shredded carrot behind. She then dropped in two plates, discarding Teddy's thrice-bitten hot dog and Denna's barely touched salad that was heavy with balsamic. She tossed her own empty plate she never had a chance to fill after contemplating if maybe she needed to eat. But no. That wasn't going to help. Her stomach growled in protest, trying to convince her otherwise. But where even picking at the contents of the table's main courses or finger-snacking on the potato chips may have been satisfying to her diminishing appetite, it wouldn't have had an effect or reversal on the needlepoint ache that was growing in her head.

Pain relievers or drinking more water was not going to help stave off the throbbing ache either. She knew.

This wasn't an ordinary headache.

The pressure was only going to build, continue to gain strength, and become overwhelming.

She had witnessed her husband's suffering.

And then…

The writing on the wall was but a matter of time.

Kelsey first noticed the sensation of a nagging tightness above her left eye just as Pete and Denna were setting out to make a trip around the lake. Her first thoughts were frantic and hobbled with dread, to stop them before they left, following the pact they made to get out once one of them became inflicted with the headache that seemed the precursor. But she ultimately held back, said she was fine. She let them go. Because she'd already overcome a similar affliction that she attributed to allergies when they all arrived. And she prayed her friends would be back quick with news of the whereabouts of her husband and Carrie, and then they would leave, together. Leave and get back to Margaret and the twins. Leave and do whatever they could to warn the world to stay away.

Stay away? Stay away from what?

Who would believe us?

As a distraction, Kelsey began cleaning up. Trying to ward her mind off the intruding and spreading and deepening invasion of pain.

For comfort, little as it would provide, she did the easy math and estimated that Ben had become plagued by his headache the second they pulled onto Bass Lane. His disappearance happened just over an hour later. By the time on her phone—just after seven (Pete mentioned the time being twenty to the hour before leaving)—Kelsey determined her headache had only been onset for about fifteen minutes.

At most she had forty-five minutes to get out.

Infected by what? she thought. *Ben's disappearance to where?*

Could it happen to me faster than it happened to Ben?

She didn't suppose and wouldn't dare assume this thing—whatever it was—worked on any consistent timetable. Carrie had only just mentioned her headache at the table minutes before she was gone.

What is doing this to us?

So many questions.

And all Kelsey had were guesses.

Nothing made sense in her head. Her thoughts were a jumble of incoherencies. Implausibilities. Hurt. Worries. Anxieties.

What's going to happen to my kids?

Ben's mother can't take care of them…

The unfortunate and worrying counterpoint: *But she'll have to.*

"I have to get out of here."

Her scattered, spiderwebbed thoughts focusing solely now on the purposes of her own preservation, her own plan of escape and getting back home to her children, Kelsey found the keys to the 4Runner on the coffee table and made sure she had her phone. The screen retained its outgoing call status of trying to connect to Ben's phone. Surely by now it was of no use. Needled with regret, Kelsey dabbed to end the call, but couldn't abandon him completely. She opened the thread of texts she shared with her husband and wrote a short message she hoped wouldn't be the last between them but, with hope dwindling, carried the weight of a goodbye.

I'm so sorry…for everything. I wish I could take it all back. I won't give up trying to find you. I love you.

A green status bar streaming left to right across the width of the screen paused at three-quarters, needing more of a signal to complete the task of sending the text. Kelsey believed once she was out beyond the perimeter of the woods her phone would easily find and link to the network. No need to wait around any longer. She considered leaving Pete and Denna a message to find on her way out the door but figured they would see the 4Runner gone and know she'd left.

"Hopefully, they'll be right behind me."

The front of her head pounding so hard the pain could melt her face, eyelids feeling weighed down, swollen and heavy, and ears feeling stuffed with cotton and ringing with the hollow gong of faraway bells, Kelsey got herself out of the lake house, across the tall grass, and into the driver's seat. She had one hand on the wheel and a finger about to depress the engine start-up when bright lights swung into view, growing on approach in her rearview mirror.

Pete and Denna.

Thank God.

Despairing and agonizing, Kelsey wanted to know if they'd found any sign of her husband or Carrie, so she waited. She waited, holding on, the pain in her head screaming, watching those two circles of expanding headlamps go shapeless and fill the mirror—filling the entire car with blinding light, becoming the sun. She smiled. Hopeless. Resigned. The very core of her mind split, fractured, and then—quickly as the overwhelming tide of agony came over her—the torment ended. The pain burned off like a fleeting mist.

Trembling in the aftermath of an adrenaline spike and a sudden sharp decline in her suffering, Kelsey's eyes spilled tears as her shaky smile flowed into a combination of wild, cackling laughter and sobs in the white fire of consuming light.

7:10 p.m.

First there was a thought.

More a color than a rational thought.

That color was warmth.

Then a shallow breath.

With that cognizance of taking a breath, a deeper sip was taken.

Air filled lungs.

Lungs expanded.

Ugh. Lungs ached.

Or maybe his chest?

Something broken.

        The air released.

           The breath completed.

    It hurt.

        Everything hurt. Like fire.

But he was breathing.

Alive.

His lips moved. Sticky. A harsh, coppery taste.

The brain computed. The brain recognized.

Blood.

His.

His name.

He was Teddy.

The brain computed some more. The brain remembered.

An accident.

A tree.

        He took regular breaths.

            Waking.

Eyes opened. Blurry.

Focusing.

The tree.

Next to him.

He lay over on a crumpled hood.

Broken glass. Broken metal.

The rest of him somewhere behind.

Also probably broken.

His legs.

He felt them. Moved them. A little.

He flexed his hands. Lifted his head. Looked around.

The woods.

A smell reached his brain.

    Hot metal.

        Oil.

He took it all in, comprehending,

        remembering.

Teddy started moving, finding resistance, finding pain, but able.

It was easier to lie still, remain where he was, but he couldn't.

He had to fight. He had to stay awake.

Hands pushed against the hood, against sharp wrinkles and cracks of metal, broken glass.

He slid himself slowly backwards, off the hood, over the steering wheel, back inside.

He dropped into the seat, body hurting, feeling like rubber, but he stayed upright.

He kept his eyes open.

Kept breathing.

Fumbling with a tingling left hand, he found the lever on the door and managed to pull hard enough to release it.

The door yawned open with a tired wail.

Teddy slithered his way out onto his feet, despite wobbly knees, surprised he could carry any of his own weight. But he managed.

Hand holding the open door for support, he took one shaky step, baby-like—reluctant but determined—over the soft, crunchy ground of old leaves and dead sticks. He took another. His progress improved. He let go of the door, took more steps on his own. Preservation and determination led him. When he could, he turned—hip screaming at him as he rotated—and inspected the wreckage.

He spoke. More of a bubbly garble.

"Whoaaaaaa."

The word wove out through swollen, gnashed, bloodied lips. Maybe a few broken teeth.

How he'd survived…Teddy couldn't guess.

Just be thankful.
Keep taking steps.
Keep moving.
Breathe.

He slide-stepped his way to the moonlit road.

He fumbled around his person, feeling all over.

Found his phone, unblemished, still in his back pocket.

A slide of his finger over the screen, a dab later, Teddy activated the flashlight, lighting a pathway to follow along the shadowy route of cracked and crumbling pavement.

He began walking, gaining stride, gaining speed, finding it a miracle his body, despite the soreness of strain and tightness and sharp little stabs here and there, felt good. Good enough to walk.

Except his head.

His head still throbbed.

7:12 p.m.

The headlights flooded over the back end of the Renmores' 4Runner, then swept left across the medley of exterior facade that was gray stone composite, red paneling, and white aluminum siding on the ranch-style lake house, shining in both bay windows, as Pete veered off Bass Lane and parked in his old spot, tire tracks still embedded in the grass. Before he could turn off the engine and unbuckle, Denna was already out and hurrying to the front door directly ahead to the right of the elbow on the L-shaped residence. By the time Pete caught up to her, she had gone out the back door and was standing in a pool of soft light granted by the motion sensor affixed just above the doorframe. She was shouting for Kelsey in such a feral way she had lost restraint, giving over to fear in place of self-control. Goose bumps rippled up Pete's arms, flaring heat into his ears, hearing Denna's unfettered shouts travel away from them and ricochet off the calm, black water.

"Where is she?"

It was a dumb question, Pete knew, but he asked it anyway because that seemed the only rational thing to say in such a fitful, terror-ridden moment. Asking was also a thin, protective barrier between a fragile hope and the horrific truth he wasn't ready to accept.

Denna turned to him, her pale skin almost washed out completely in the light. She appeared to Pete as wraithlike, almost glowing with a white aura. Haunted, for sure. Her eyes were notable for being red-rimmed and glassy. Her toughened demeanor relenting, exposed by the loss and having to comp to it. "She's gone."

Pete wanted to protest. Felt a stirring of buzzing bees in his chest that was the withheld opposition to rattle off any number of defenses, excuses, possibilities to how and why that claim was simply untrue. He wanted to counter that Kelsey hadn't disappeared, not like Ben and not like Carrie, that she was probably scared (as they all were) and trying to get out and was waiting for them somewhere, because finding a rational response was anyone's natural inclination. But that flimsy rebuttal was just as dumb as his question posing where Kelsey was at. He knew. Pete tamped the denials that were choking him up. He knew.

He asked, "So, what do we do?"

Another dumb question, but he needed to hear Denna say it.

He needed that confirmation as he stepped down out of the doorway and looked out, a kickup breeze carrying the scents of pine and sweet dirt across the lake, chilly on his face, able to spot small lights out of the darkness through the whispering leaves and waving branches and the clearing of Echo Lake. Lights on sheds, on the backs of houses, along the handrails on the docks, all around the fringes of the lake that were on timers, or were solar, or were simply left on with no one left to turn them off, waiting for the bulbs to die, visible now in the late evening. Lights at the near dozen homes that, they both knew, now sat in their different states of unfinished stasis, abandoned. Meals served and left to spoil. Repairs not finished. Laundry half folded. Stories and laughter and last sentiments of love maybe shared, maybe not, before the residents of each home vanished. Missing to God knows where.

With nothing else to offer, Denna succumbed to their powerlessness and said, "We go."

7:15 p.m.

They were back in the Mazda. Denna peered out the passenger window to the empty front seat of the 4Runner next to them as Pete threw the car in Reverse. She knew. In her thoughts as she mourned her friend, she thought about Ben and Kelsey's little ones—the boys, Ryan and Ben Jr., and Margaret…

Oh, poor Margaret.

The three will be inconsolable when their parents don't come home, but with the boys being so young, their memories of this time will fade easier and quicker (if that was any consolation prize). Maybe. They'll have a better chance of healing, moving on, for a while anyway. The loss won't really sink in until they are older and can process the magnitude of such a core event in their lives. Margaret, on the other hand, is old enough that the exact moment of learning the awful news won't be a clear memory forever, but she'll have the scar of her parents going missing embedded in her heart for the rest of her life.

"I've never been happy about not having a child until right now."

Pete finished backing them onto Bass Lane and gunned the car forward, pitching them both back into their seats with a heavy jostle. "What's that?"

"Children," said Denna over the growl of the engine being pushed. "I had been hoping Teddy and I would—" She stopped herself when the words wouldn't come easy, and it was also then when she realized. "I'm sorry. I'm sorry about Ava."

Pete's lower jaw flexed and shifted in a poor attempt to conceal his emotion. He kept his eyes, determined though revealing his heartache and worries penetrating his armor, on the road. His mouth formed a tight, thin line as he tried to remain even warily positive. "It's all right. I'm…I'm gonna get back to her." He repeated this line, "gonna get back to her," softer the second time, as if he was also trying to convince himself and not just make the promise to Denna.

The headlights bathed the stretch of deteriorating road, flanked by swaying trees reaching out with their hundreds of bent arms and thousands of crooked fingers that had taken on a more oppressive scene now that they were eager to escape. Bass Lane, in all its crumbling infamy, went on into the dark horizon, an endless, sinister corridor that was pushing inward, enclosing them. Pete wouldn't have been shocked if the end never came, if they were on this road forever.

In his thoughts he swore a promise to his daughter, and then one to his sister. Pete loved his sister Becky, but he wasn't about to make Becky an aunt *and* a stepparent if he could help it. In the first Last Will and Testament Pete and Carrie had drafted—this on the advice of their own parents following Ava's birth—it was a fact they decreed that Becky would take guardianship of their daughter in the event of an early demise, but that was for reasons more sentimental than practical. Pete's sister wasn't yet ready for that responsibility. Carrie predicted that even this single overnight would prove too much, and Becky would call on her and Pete's parents for help. As a single person, Becky was just fine—she had her ducks in a row. But the life of parenthood and its acquired responsibilities remained elusive, concepts out of reach. Becky would have to change her lifestyle and perspective, and Pete knew she wasn't ready to make those detours and sacrifices. So he made his promises and kept them at the front of his mind. That he was going to get out, that he was going home. His daughter was the fuel keeping him striving onward after Carrie was taken—

Yeah, he thought, *taken…that's what's happening out here…something is taking people…but why? For what?*

—and he would never stop searching for his wife, and he felt tremendous pangs of guilt and anger for leaving, but he knew Carrie would want this—

"Pete—*stop*!"

Denna's cry ringing his ears, snapping him out of his own head, Pete stomped the brake pedal to the floor. The Mazda responded in kind, back end swerving, fishtailing as the tires ground into the decrepit pavement. They screeched to a halt, a cloud of smoked rubber rising in their wake. Pete saw now what Denna already had. Someone walking, limping, shuffling toward them right down the middle of the road. Had Pete not stopped, this person would have been reduced to a quarter-mile smear of limbs and liquid permanently pressed into the cracks on the road.

Denna fumbled for the door latch. "Teddy!"

Pete learned the alarm in her voice came from the numerous injuries Teddy was now carrying with him. With Teddy basked in the headlights that he now shielded his eyes from, it was clear from his grease-smudged, dirty, torn clothing; the gashes and scrapes on his arms, elbows, knees, and shins; the streaks of blood and swelling on his hands (the glints of what could have been sparkles of glass in his palms); and what could be seen of his shadowed face that he'd suffered a substantial incident.

Leaving the engine running and lights on, Pete scrambled out to help, getting to Teddy just as he collapsed into his wife's arms.

7:21 p.m.

"Come on, buddy, stay with us."

They managed to use Teddy's falling momentum to guide his folding body to the pavement, laying him out prone. Denna knelt down, providing her lap to cushion and prop his head. She combed the wisps of his sweat-slicked, blood-matted hair away from his brow so his wounds could be inspected under the searching flashlight of their phones. Nothing appeared too deep. Maybe one would require glue or stitching, but most (luckily) were superficial. There was a lot of blood because head wounds bleed a lot. Pete applied round after round of gentle rapid slaps to Teddy's stubbled cheeks, keeping him awake and aware when his breathing took on a light snore. Pete shined the light of his phone in Teddy's eyes, noticing the slow transitions of his pupils. He was no doctor, but a concussion (at the very least) seemed prevalent enough to diagnose.

"Hey, look at me," Pete said, and Teddy's eyes performed a roll around before coming back to lock on him. "Can you tell me how many fingers I'm holding up?"

Teddy echoed, "Can you tell me how many I'm holding up?" and displayed his scratched-up middle finger.

Pete looked to Denna and both agreed. "He's fine."

"What happened?" Denna asked.

"I…" Teddy rolled his head side to side, ear to ear, from one of his wife's thighs to the other, leaving residue smudges of sweat and blood on her pale legs, eyes blinking, eyes fluttering, eyes closing. Pete scanned over him again with his light, gently feeling around, squeezing and turning limbs, checking for any other injuries more serious than the cuts and abrasions sustained. "It just came on so fast. My head… Went off the road." He chuckled. "Sorry, babe. Time for a new car. Better…ask TechWorld for a raise." He laughed at whatever in his broken summary he found funny. As a result, the wound at his hairline just off-center began to run with fresh blood again.

"What do we do?" Denna asked Pete, relaying none of the humor her husband was enjoying.

Pete said, "We've got to get him to a hospital."

"Oh man, you guys should totally see your faces." Teddy burst out with hitching giggles.

The long, telling glance between Pete and Denna displayed a greater concern, communicating a grim worry that Teddy might have suffered some kind of internal head injury that needed immediate attention.

"Should we even be moving him?" Denna asked.

"Probably not, but what choice do we have? I mean…we can lay him in the back seat and go—"

Another titter from Teddy, the kind that came across as a rejection to their developing plans. To further emphasize in a cartoonish way, he put a thumbs-down and blew a long raspberry that catapulted spittle into the air, landing on his cheeks and Denna's legs.

"You can't," Teddy said, getting his laughter under control. "We can't… go." His *go* was elongated, tapering off. The fingers on his right hand danced a flutter, composing the trailing off of his voice.

Pete asked, "Why not?"

The mask of tragic comedy that had been expressed on Teddy's face withdrew. The wrinkles of his smile alongside his mouth and the crow's feet accentuated by his eyes that also marked his giddiness smoothened out, vanishing. What took over, possessing Teddy, was a complete look of coherence that hadn't been there since Pete and Denna found him stumbling his way on the road. His voice was normal, lucid. His head wound leaked a new singular dark line that rolled over his left temple, headed toward his ear. "Because it won't let us."

Denna leaned over him, her perspective of her husband had him upside down. His eyes rolled upward, far as they could go without disappearing to all whites, finding her. "What won't let us?"

Those eyes of his softened, losing their focus. Though his irises and dilated pupils remained on her, Teddy was now seeing through her to somewhere distant. Somewhere beyond. "Whatever's keeping us here."

Pete dug out his keys. They rattled together on the carabiner in his unsteady hands. "I can go." Despite the hastiness of the moment, he mustered up some confidence in the plan that formed in his head. "I can get down to the end of the road till I get a signal and call for an ambulance."

Denna wondered, "What about us?"

A slight titter burst out of Teddy, eerily intruding on the quiet, lingering uncertainty brewing beyond them. An unusual quiet that also invaded the surrounding woods. "It won't let you get that far."

Pete ignored his wounded friend. "I won't be long."

Denna raised her brows. "What if he's right?"

Shrugging, Pete didn't have any contingencies, and there wasn't time to debate. It was now all or nothing. "I don't know."

Worry creased Denna's forehead. "We can't call for an ambulance."

Teddy interjected, "I am right. Trust me."

Pete asked, "Why not?"

"If he's right and we can't get out," said Denna as calmly as she could, "then bringing in more people will also put them in danger."

Teddy pointed in the air with his right hand in the shape of a gun, producing a clicking noise with his bloodied tongue. "Bingooo."

"So, now what?" Denna asked.

Pete paced the broken road. The heels of his sneakers scuffed the concrete. "Give me a second."

Teddy scoffed. "None of us are getting out."

Denna pleaded against their helplessness. "We can't just stay here—we have to try something!"

Pete continued walking in tight circles. "I'll think of something. Just give me a minute."

"You guys ever wonder why there are flotation devices on airplanes?" pondered Teddy.

Denna felt herself losing a grip on the moment, perhaps her sanity as well. "What?"

Ceasing his pacing, Pete's face lit up as he clapped his hands in triumph. "Okay. I think I have an idea."

Teddy wondered aloud, "Shouldn't they have parachutes instead?"

Again, Pete ignored his friend's ramblings, which spoke a lot to Teddy's sustained injuries but was a matter to be dealt with afterward. "You said your head started hurting all of a sudden while you were driving?"

Teddy replied, "I mean, what are the chances of a plane always flying over water?"

Denna was losing patience. "Teddy!"

Pete resumed his pacing, but slower. The walking back and forth was helping him expound the jumbled solution in his thoughts. "What if…what if whatever is around us is like some kind of…some kind of force field, right? And…and trying to speed through it causes the headache to come on really strong? You know? Disorientating. What if I just try driving as far as I can and then…walking out? Maybe that will work. What do you think?"

It was a while before Denna answered. "I mean…it's worth a shot?"

Teddy added, "You sound like the person who thought it was a good idea to put flotation devices on airplanes."

Gripping his keys tight in a sturdy fist that flexed blue veins and a protrusion of white through his knuckles, Pete nodded, affirmed. "Okay." He stood up, dusted his hands off on his shorts, sounding more determined. "If I get out and get a signal, I'll call an ambulance to meet us on the road. If that works, I'll come back to get you and we'll leave the same way."

"What about us right now?" Denna asked. "What if something happens to you? We won't have a car, and…" Continuing to wipe beneath her eyes, continuing to fight the urges to scream and cry, and submitting to being thrown off-kilter, losing her mental balance and orientation, Denna regarded her husband; everything horrific and telling she wanted to say about his condition was there to be implied. "He needs somewhere to rest."

At a shortage for answers, Pete squeezed wrinkles into his brow and clawed fingers through his beard. Urgency was the first order of business, but she was right—he couldn't leave them stranded in the middle of the road in the dark.

"I'll take you both back to the house. We'll get him situated. Then I'll go."

Given it was the best of crappy options all around, Denna agreed.

Teddy lifted his head off her lap. "You guys…" He sounded coherent. "I think I might've been in an accident."

7:53 p.m.

To keep the amount of light dim inside so as not to further aggravate her husband's possible sustained head injury and maintain his comfort for as long as Pete would be gone, Denna switched off the small but brilliant glass lamp on the red wooden stand beside the couch after lighting two candles she located on a shelf in the small closet, setting one on the coffee table and one on the counter in the kitchen space. To her disfavor, the candles were scented. The green one housed in a jar on the coffee table was called Holiday Pine on its wraparound label, and the burnt-orange one in the kitchen was dubbed Autumn Spice. At the moment, Teddy didn't object to the flickering candlelight or the mix of aromas filling the living room as he had slipped into a doze moments after Pete set him on the couch. He had remained alert and coherent throughout being carried and laid across the back seat in the Mazda for their trip back to the lake house, teasing Pete upon entering.

"Aw, you're carrying me over the threshold."

Not a minute after being set down on the couch, a blanket spread over him to stave off the risk of shock, Teddy was softly sawing wood. Rummaging around, Denna found a bottle of 70 percent rubbing alcohol along with some gauze pads and bandages of various sizes in a drawer beneath the bathroom sink. She used the pads to dab and clean up the two dozen scrapes and cuts on her husband's face and neck and the ones she could find on his hands, then bandaged the ones she thought needed covering. If there had been any sting due to the use of alcohol, it wasn't enough to rouse her husband. When finished, she rose to full height beside the couch, observing her work while biting a thumbnail, monitoring Teddy's condition—his light, rhythmic breathing—still unable to shake off the distress of their helplessness.

"Don't let him sleep too long," Pete advised. "Keep waking him every few minutes."

They stood about ten feet apart—Pete at the front door, hand on the knob, looking back at her over his shoulder—but in the freeform of moving shadows and dancing orange firelight chasing each other for purchase over the floors and across the walls it seemed a far greater void of dark emptiness between them.

He wanted to say more but didn't know what that should be.

He wanted to cross the plain of space that separated them, provide some kind of comfort, steal some for himself even to counter the fear of going on alone, everything dependent on him, but to cross that barrier felt inappropriate. His own wife hadn't even been gone two hours.

Aware this could be the last time he saw and stood in the presence of another human being (and why did that feel fated to be Denna of all people?) Pete kept himself composed as best he could against falling into the trap of desperate impulses.

"I'll be as quick as I can," he said, holding on to that mustered strength. He told himself he could fall apart outside, when he'd be by himself, but not here, not right now.

Denna nodded, looked like she wanted to say more, and he wished she would—*Say anything, please*—but she didn't.

Rather than drag out the inevitable and risk her catching a glimpse of his vulnerabilities and eroding bravado, which would reveal themselves the longer he procrastinated at the door, Pete stepped out into the cooling night. He jogged to his car, took a steadying breath before keying the ignition, looked at himself in the mirror to locate and regain some confidence (also really glad he didn't say something back at the house he might come to regret if he and Denna and Teddy actually got through this predicament), and got back out onto the road. Though Teddy's well-being ticked along to the running clock, Pete followed Bass Lane not to the left and immediately toward its exit out of the woods, but to the right on its designated one-way path that wrapped around the lake. He justified that this excursion for his curiosity would only add an additional five minutes.

At each of the eleven other homes around the now unseen bed of water, only two others besides the neighbor with the overflowing kiddie pool had lights on inside. Pete laid on the horn at each one then parked in the road and ran to bang on the doors, making such a noise that couldn't be ignored. No one answered. He didn't feel it necessary to waste further time breaking into these homes. He already knew what he would find inside if he did.

No one.

We're the last ones.

Completing the loop around Echo Lake, he looked to the L-shaped lake house right at the point of entry onto the single lane road where Denna and Teddy were inside (seeing the blinking candlelight in both of the bay windows out front) and hoped this slight detour hadn't cost them before applying added pressure on the gas and speeding down the straightaway.

"Here we go." Pete continued talking to himself, getting louder, pumping himself up for the first inklings of pressure building in his head that he anticipated. "Let's do this, you bitch."

Retracing the already taken route, Pete alternated between biting the left and right sides of his tongue as he passed the spot where they had come upon a staggering Teddy, then the area where the severed ash tree had fallen, once blocking their path and now reduced to two halves moved off to the shoulders, and he kept flooring the gas. The needle for the speedometer passed by fifty on its clockwise sweep, holding steady around seventy. The tires rumbled over the uneven pavement, vibrating the steering wheel and shimmying the seats. The headlights shone on the monotonous scenery of trees and crackled road and more trees. Occasionally, he'd see a small, ghost-white moth or a mayfly, but not more than a few. At about a mile, something flagged Pete's eye off the road to the right, bringing him to lay weight on the brakes. The speedometer needle swung back to hover just under thirty miles per hour as he caught sight of the front end of a four-seater that used to resemble the Meers's Jeep Wrangler, now almost unrecognizable and folded in, wrapped around the thick base of an ash tree.

"Jesus. How the hell did he walk away from that?"

By the ragged hole and amount of glass piled on the crumpled hood right in front of the driver's seat, Pete imagined Teddy had been launched right through, which accounted for the presumed concussion and many cuts and scrapes.

Pete thought it was a damn stroke of luck, maybe even divine intervention, that Teddy didn't slice his neck open and bleed out in seconds.

If he gets out of this, dude needs to get himself a lotto ticket.
Hell, we all should.

The car drifted slowly by the scene. Having been surpassed by the headlights, the debris and ruin were soon swallowed up in the dark.

"Keep going," Pete told himself, ushering on. "It hasn't gotten you yet."

Fascinating—perhaps morbidly, impressively fascinating—as the wreckage was and that Teddy had walked away from it (though he hadn't exactly fared untouched), Pete decided against loitering. There was nothing more to see, plus he hadn't been affected yet—even shook his head to double-check—and wasn't about to start pushing his own luck, which history had proven to be questionable.

Except this time, he did feel something.

A nagging pinspot, weak and embedded so deep under the surface it was hardly perceptible, had begun pressing toward the surface, persisting about an inch above his right eye, sending out waves of its warning radio signals now that it had been detected.

"Just eyestrain from the dark. Trying to see."

His doubting inner voice told him that wasn't true.

"I can keep going."

His inner voice told him to stop and check to see if he had a signal.

"I'm almost out."

But he wasn't.

Not near enough.

And the pain dialed up.

"No, no, no."

He squeezed his eyes shut to ward off the tightening pressure clutching his skull, grinding it excruciatingly slowly, rendering bone into dust. Upon realizing the mistake of blinding himself to the road, Pete forced his eyes back open. He began to swerve to straighten out. The pain had become so great, so consuming and loud, he could no longer hear his thoughts, felt delirious, his stomach souring and puckering and threatening to betray him. He could no longer navigate the straightforward path. He had enough sound mind and wherewithal to take his foot off the gas, allowing the car to coast for as long as it could. With no one around, he was free to howl out his agony with one hand on the wheel guiding as best he could, the other hand squeezing all around his head to isolate and minimize the nauseating strobes of pain.

The needle on the speedometer slid counterclockwise, back from twenty to ten to five to zero.

The front right tire dipped into a sizable pothole on Bass Lane, and the car stopped rolling.

Pete hissed each breath, dragging streams of icy air in through the gaps between clenched teeth. His head hurt so bad he couldn't determine if no longer moving was making it better or not. Maybe there was some nugget of truth to that weird theory about the rate of motion having some impact on the effect whatever field existed around them was outputting. Regardless, he was still there, still breathing. Nothing else had happened to him.

"Guess this is my stop."

Pete pulled the latch and kicked the driver's side door open. The crisp night air full of bug song provided no relief, in fact may have exacerbated his sensitivities, causing him to notice each tireless throb against his temples, each resounding bell in the depths of his ears. Every movement standing up outside of the car welcomed more crippling, icy drumbeats into his brain. His stomach gave a nauseous lurch as a wave of heat pulsed off his damp skin.

He swallowed to gain his bearings and keep everything in his stomach right where it was. A check of his phone showed it was connected to the LTE network, but a dial next to the acronym kept spinning.

"Looks like I'm walking from here."

The reach of his headlights, left on so that he could see through the dark, looked to end after about a hundred yards or so down the broken road. Pete hoped to make it to the edge of the light, maybe a little farther. Then he'd check his phone again.

But he knew Teddy was right. Had come to relinquish his own denials as he began a slow walk that was more about skidding his feet along the pavement than actual steps.

The pain was only going to get worse as he pushed onward toward the boundaries of the woods. The invisible force field (as he considered it) would become more restrictive. He wasn't going to be allowed to leave. It would eventually take him, like it had his wife. Like it had the others.

Pete accepted his new responsibility.

This was no longer a rescue mission to get out.

He wasn't getting home to Ava.

He needed to warn others to stay away.

8:04 p.m.

The only thing to do was wait.

Denna paced the living room, looked out the windows to nothing but confined darkness, wandered into the kitchenette, picked at open bags of chips and other snacks left on the counter, and then felt guilty about it because, despite her growling stomach, this seemed a most unsuitable time to be munching. Her husband lay asleep, so she took a gander at the time on her phone and set a reminder to wake him in five minutes just to be safe, in the very likely event he had suffered a brain injury in his accident. For the moment he rested peacefully, still breathing, and his wounds remained dry. The strip of gauze she'd bandaged high on his forehead at the hairline had red on it, but the layers hadn't been soaked all the way through. His most serious wound seemed to be clotting, or at least slowing down.

No telling how long Pete would be gone, no way to know if he would be successful trying to leave or get help. No promise he was coming back. Everything lingered, uncertain.

"Eh. Fuck it."

She shoved her hand deep into a bag of Chex Mix that was calling out to her, the open end like a wide mouth taunting, begging. She was going to eat her feelings. There was no other available comfort. If she'd been given a preference, she would have rather demolished a package of Double Stuf Oreos (her mouth watered at the thought of twisting off the tops of two then combining the other ends to make her own Quadruple Stuf creation). Alas, beggars can't be choosers, so Chex Mix it was. At this point it would go down just as well.

Under no one's watchful eye, she shoved handful after handful into her mouth without shame. Any crumbs and pieces of loose breadsticks, rye chips, and broken Chex pieces that missed and fell to the countertop and the floor were left willfully neglected. Denna continued her binging, surprised by her own level of intake. She dug an alcoholic lemonade-flavored seltzer out of the fridge, popped the top, and chased down the saltiness with thirstful gulps. A very throaty, unladylike belch fizzed its way up and loudly exited, which made her laugh.

For 11.2 seconds she forgot all about everything going wrong. Her stomach felt full, bloated, satisfied. The quick draining of the adult beverage sent a happy little buzz bubbling through her head. Then an alarm started ringing on her phone.

Time to wake Teddy.

8:10 p.m.

She knelt down next to the couch, remorseful she had to disturb him.

Awake, her husband could be riddled with pain. A hastened heart rate would pump his blood faster. Any careless, restless movements would cause his deeper wounds to reopen and be allowed to ooze and leak. Asleep he was calm, motionless, at peace. Asleep, his body was better able to heal itself. Asleep he wasn't living this nightmare.

But if Pete was right—if Teddy was dealing with serious head trauma—a prolonged sleep could prove fatal.

Neither choice was preferential, unfortunately.

Denna reached a hand out to lay on him, to gently nudge him, but shy of contact she stopped herself.

She weighed the alternative.

Their predicament for the time being was inescapable. Their outcomes were determined, fates sealed. What gain could be earned from waking Teddy when their eventuality was but a matter of time? Did she really want to put him through the suffering and the worry? Having him aware and present for the end felt like a cruel decision to make on his behalf without his consent. Wouldn't it be better, humane, if he were allowed to meet his end while already at rest? Wouldn't she want that painless drifting off into the sweet release of oblivion for herself if she had the choice?

How could she rob him of that painless, fearless end?

Denna withdrew her hand.

She used that same hand to wipe the birthing tears. To cover her mouth so her sobbing wouldn't disturb him.

Denna decided she didn't want to watch.

She spun to sit on the floor, her back pressed against the stiff front end of the couch. She took up the Holiday Pine candle on the coffee table and extinguished it with a curt blow, cutting the living room to pitch-dark. A stiff punch of aroma wafted off the rising smoke of the melting wick. The end would come, come for them both, but at least Teddy would remain oblivious.

Until he spoke.

"Smells like Christmas."

Denna laughed, a simultaneous laugh of weighty relief and sadness.

"What's happening?" he asked.

Denna bowed her head to rest on her drawn-up, bundled knees, hearing in his question a confusion of why all the pain, why him. She also heard when he lost that punch-drunk ramble to his tone. She reached a hand back and found one of his atop the blanket to squeeze. He had considerable strength in return, his grip holding on, not yet ready to let go.

"What is doing this to us?"

She answered in a throat-tightened rasp, "I don't know."

Teddy took a long, deep inhale through his nose. "My head…" She heard the stifled grimace in the release of his exhale behind her. He was trying to mask what ailed him. "Denna. It's happening."

"What?"

"I…I can feel it."

There was awareness, comprehension, a wonder, and a finality in his conviction.

She squeezed his hand harder. Tears freely splashed down her face.

"Teddy?"

"It's okay."

The clarity, how at peace he sounded, only wrecked her further. A complete succumbing to the pull, slowly whisking him off.

"I'm sorry," he said. "I know you wanted children."

Denna kept her hold on him as he did his best to muffle every groan and wince.

"I'm not afraid," he whispered. "Don't be afraid."

He uttered another grit of discomfort.

"It's not so bad."

His last words.

Denna went from holding his hand to holding nothing.

Her hand fell through where he should have been, passed through without a hint in the air of what previously was, and landed on the stiff cushion of the couch. She ran a gentle sweep of her warm palm over the place where her husband's body once laid, finding only the depressions that had already begun to rise and reform. Erasing his presence. His existence.

She cried.

8:15 p.m.

His progress had narrowed to a slow shuffle, skittering both feet along, the bottoms of his sneakers dragging on the loose stones over the fissured pavement. At the fringe of the headlights' reach, nearing the cusp between the remaining faded light and where absolute dark took over the world, where his shadow once stretched out before him had, minus the portion of his legs below the kneecaps, vanished into the unseen void, Pete checked his phone. At first the brightness of the screen was too much for his eyes to handle, stabbing through his pulsating skull. A warm and nauseous snake slithered around in his belly. He managed to lower the brightness level by squinting at the screen kept off-center of his line of vision and dabbing and sliding through the settings. When able to examine the screen closely, he found there was a network connection.

Thank Christ.

Only a bar, one out of four, was filled to indicate the solid link. No longer was an "in progress" dial spinning.

Pete stopped right where he was. Looking down, he could barely make out his feet standing in the shallows of an invading pitch-black tide.

Fuck, his head hurt. There was no telling how much farther before the end of Bass Lane outside of the woods—could have been fifty feet, could have been five thousand—but that didn't matter. Pete didn't know if he could complete one more step, not without throwing up from wave after wave of disorienting hot sickness pushing through him over the persistent ache that throbbed in his head. The pressure was so bad the old metal fillings in his back teeth hurt. The bridge of his nose hurt. His ears rang with a steady, hollow gong that was traveling miles through tunnel space to reach him. Every swallow to rid his mouth of building saliva sent an excruciating bullet of flexing muscles up from his jaw through the top of his skull.

He'd rather die.

He'd rather lie down right here in the middle of the road at the ass-end of nowhere (what he now considered the antithesis of Disney World with Echo Lake being the Shittiest Place on Earth) and let it be over.

But first…

But first.

He entered his six-digit pin to unlock the phone, messing up twice before putting in real concentration to not make a third mistake and lock himself out of his phone for the next half hour (and grateful he didn't have to draw a pattern to unlock the screen). He couldn't make it another two minutes like this, let alone a half hour. Those few seconds spent engaging on the screen he paid dearly for, catching a tightening of the vice that felt like it was going to spit his eyeballs out of his skull. Pete steadied his breathing, sucked in a deep whistle of air, and willed himself to hold it together just long enough to make the call. After opening his contacts, he quickly started spelling Becky's name, got her at the top of the results, and immediately dabbed to begin the call.

He only continued looking at the screen long enough to put the call on speaker and see the time begin to run. The call connected. He moaned out the last of his earned agonies and then sighed a garbled thank-you to whatever higher power allowed his call to go through.

The line rang once.

"Come on, answer."

The line rang twice.

"Shiiiit. Don't do this."

A third time.

"Come onnnn."

At the end of the fourth ring, the tone clipped. Pete brought the phone closer to his face.

"Becky? Hello?"

Pete's sister answered.

"Hi, this is Rebecca. I can't come to my phone right now. But if you leave your name and number and a brief message, I'll get back to you as soon as possible. Thanks."

Pete didn't have time to register and dwell on the missed opportunity of not getting to speak to his sister and hear her voice beyond the stiff intonations of her recorded message, to hear his daughter one last time. Before he could comprehend the weightless feeling in his chest and stomach from that eternal loss, before he could conjure what to say at all, the inbox messaging service beeped to begin its recording.

Too many jumbled words in his head, none coming out of his mouth.

Speak! he demanded of himself. *There's no time.*

Time. Such a precious thing.

Always moving, hardly noticed until it becomes precious.

Say something!

Pete closed his eyes, tried to picture through the pain, tried to imagine his sister and his daughter, tried to erase all sense of anguish from his voice.

"Beck…um. Uh. You're, um, you're probably with Ava right now. Maybe…maybe she woke up, and, um, you had to comfort her."

Get it together, man.

This is what they'll remember.

"When you get this message…I-I want you to listen closely. Something's happened. To me and Carrie. To everyone up here. We don't know what it is, if it's a sickness or…or something else."

"Whatever you do, don't come here. Don't bring Ava here, ever. You both stay away. Stay as far away as you can. Nobody can come here. I wish this was a joke, I really do, but it's not. It's not. You really have to listen to me."

Pete could only imagine his available time with the recording was almost up and that the voicemail would disconnect. He told himself to get the rest of it out.

"I hate doing this. Please. Please. Take care of my daughter. You're responsible now. You've got to do the right things for Ava."

He lowered the phone to compose himself, not wanting his struggles, his despair, to play out on the message. No doubt, in time, Ava would hear this, too.

"This next part, it's for you, Ava. Know that Mommy and Daddy loved you more than anything. I dreamt of you. Long before you were born, I had dreams of you. You look just like your mom—I want you to know that.

Which, if you were going to get your looks from one of us, you dodged a real bullet."

Gotta end it now. While you can.

"It's time for me to go, kiddo. I'll never stop dreaming of you. Never."

Now that he had said it, he could imagine a growing Ava through the years, see her one day sitting on her bed listening to his words when she became old enough to understand. His heart wanted to continue spilling out, emptying every last love note to her. He wished to keep speaking to her, giving Ava all the advice and wisdom of a father to his daughter, but Pete was obsessively conscious of the connection severing, about the message being cut off. He also decided it best to end with the utmost honesty. He would indeed dream of Ava right through the last moments.

Difficult as the choice was, and as much as he despised the choice to be made, he pressed the red button on his screen to finish the call.

He wept, with no concern of anyone or anything hearing him.

Not an owl, not a frog, not a hungry mosquito, nothing gave its response.

All that remained of Pete's desire was lying down in the road and bringing on the inevitable.

Powerless to the affliction in his head and the anguish consuming his heart, the latter harder to cope with, he dropped to his knees on the pavement. He let go of his phone. The device bounced and landed screen side up, its black screen reflecting the sprinkling of stars and radiant glow of moonlight.

"Just…just do it already."

He extended both arms welcoming, hands open, palms upward, bowing his head. A sacrificial gesture.

"Get it over with."

But the longer he remained posed for the end to sweep him away, the quicker he learned mercy was not coming. Not at his beckoning. Not on his time. Not when he was ready.

Pete looked back to the car. The warm illuminance of the headlights—two eyes in the shroud of dark—stared at him. Eyes that held him. Eyes that judged him.

Or was it Pete, judging himself?

You can't throw away whatever you have left.

Those lights seemed so far away. Barely touching him. So far away.

8:47 p.m.

Inside her purse, within her wallet, Denna scavenged for pictures. From one of the few hidden pockets of her wallet, behind where her various cards were held, she managed to find a short, crinkled roll of drunken photo booth snaps of her and Teddy. They had been taken years ago on a late-night boardwalk excursion to the bars and an arcade in Seaside Heights, New Jersey. She forgot she had kept it. The only other photo to be found was her driver's license. Not one she cared for.

    Denna examined the half dozen thumbnail pics of their much younger selves—the overexaggerated, inebriated smiles and squinty, light-sensitive eyes and the kiss they shared in the last frame—and then laid both the roll and the license on the coffee table. She harbored the tragedy that those two in the pictures had no idea about what lay ahead. That they believed they had a long life of happiness and marital bliss ahead, still young enough to feel invincible, their bond unbreakable, when in fact there would be encounters with kryptonite, all while an hourglass kept track of their depleting time and was, back then, three-quarters down. The only other photos she had were the ones that resided on her phone, which she also set on the table after removing the passcode prompt. No use leaving behind something no one could get into, if it ever gets recovered.

    Rummaging around the open layout of the lake house afterward, she found a magnetic 5 x 8 light blue legal pad that had a ribboned header reading GROCERY LIST on the face of the fridge and a dust-covered coffee cup on top which she fished out a black BIC ballpoint pen from a menagerie of pens and different-length pencils.

    Situating herself back at the coffee table, centered along the top line on the pad, she wrote the date and then the words *Amongst the missing* in short, fancy swirls. She dropped down two spaces (as her English teachers had always taught her) and, starting from the left margin, wrote the name *Ben Renmore*. She followed this by writing his age and a few short descriptors.

Loving husband and father. Talked endlessly about his kids.

Giving each their own space on the page, she did the same next for Kelsey Renmore (*Loving wife and mother. Great friend. Proud mama.*) and for Carrie Turnbull (*Glowing new mommy. Full of life and love.*), but then felt an apprehension, an aching in her hand, and a chest-tightening attack of sorrow and unease when forming the letters to spell out *Teddy Meers*.

Though she had been present, hypervigilant of the unavoidable final moments between them, and all but witnessed by touch her husband's vanishing, the inclusion of Teddy's name with the others on the list became another insurmountable task and acceptance of everything she'd lost. And one more unnecessary reminder of her fate.

But she managed it. Through hot, watery eyes she paid no mind to as they ran free, and with a hand that she steadied through sheer will, Teddy's name (albeit with a few crooked letters and connections) appeared number four on the list. In the following after a gap, she noted his age and then wrote, simply, *A good man.*

She wiped away the slick of her sorrows and dried her face. When it came to listing the fifth amongst their group, Denna paused, tapping the tip of the pen on the surface of the coffee table, never minding the shallow divots being made into the soft wood, debating whether to write her own name next or Pete's.

That's when the front door opened into the living room, and out of the night Pete stepped inside. By the frazzled, exhausted look on his face, she could tell he had been through a lot, and she was quite certain she looked to him like a mirror of just about the same.

There was comfort and ease in not being alone at the end of all things.

8:55 p.m.

"I didn't think I'd see you again." She wasn't apologetic in her bluntness. Didn't feel appropriate to be anything less than completely open and honest given the unknown amount of sand remaining in their respective hourglasses.

Pete didn't say anything right away, almost seeming to digest the meaning of her words, coming to terms with the inflexibility of their destiny, turning over in his head how it all had come down to this, to them. Then, finally, he said, "You almost didn't."

They remained not speaking, her watching him as he came away from the door and made a deliberately slow walk to the matching living room chair beside the couch. How he gave a passing glance at the couch and saw only a wrinkled blanket spread over the otherwise reformed cushions. The subtle dejection of realization and grief in his face followed. He sat down, at first rigid, hunched slightly forward, then it looked like he forced himself to relax into the backing, releasing a long, exasperated sigh that was all but succumbing. Pete massaged wrinkles into his bald head. Slowly, he ran a hand over his mouth and over his beard, staring at a fixed point somewhere low on the far side of the room.

"I'm sorry," he said. That apology carried the weight and burden of not just what happened to Teddy, but everything they had been through in the last few hours.

Denna simply nodded her gratitude. "You didn't get out."

Pete closed his eyes, a defeated gesture that confirmed no. "I did get a signal. It was weak, but I think it might've worked."

He didn't sound convinced, and hope was in short supply.

"I got a little farther than Teddy, but…the pain was just…"

"It's okay."

"I, um…I started walking back and…I decided if it didn't get better, I was going to get in the car and just gun it at all costs. Take my chances. But then it started clearing, and…I chickened out. The headache went away the closer I got back to here, so…" He shrugged in a way that proclaimed *what can ya do, ya know?* "I figured there was no reason to go through it alone. Or…leave you alone."

Denna cut a frown. "Inevitably, one of us will."

Pete agreed. "True."

"I was making a list. Felt like the right thing to do. Something to do, I guess. I was getting stir crazy. Needed the distraction. Don't know if anyone will ever find it and be able to do anything with it. Didn't know if I was going to be adding your name or not."

He sat up in the chair to look over the brief descriptions scrawled on the small pad.

"For me, can you put down 'More muscular than Chris Hemsworth, and with better hair'?" He said this while running a hand over his shorn head.

Denna eked out a polite laugh. Inklings of a smile made their first appearance since…well, hell, since everything began.

"All right," Pete compromised, more or less to keep some humor between them at such a hopeless time. "I'll settle with 'World's Coolest Dad.'"

Her spunky smile stretched wider on one side, revealing little divots aside the bridge of her scrunched, freckled nose. "You got it."

Pete noticed the roll of photo booth pictures and Denna's license also on the table and examined them in question.

"Seems when…it happens…everything on us goes away too. Clothes. Jewelry. I realized Teddy's wallet was in his pocket and that got me thinking about pictures. This was all I had to let anyone know we were here."

Reaching into his back pocket, Pete produced his own beat-up brown leather bifold and dug through all the flaps and pockets. He laid his own New York State-issued driver's license on the tabletop. He used to think people who carried around pictures of their spouses in their purses or wallets were weird, but those thoughts (inspired by recent events) were now quickly reversed.

Next, he plunked a Dunkin' gift card down next to his license. "I have no idea what's left on that, but it's not like I'll be using it. Maybe someone someday can get themselves a nice little caramel latte mochaccino on me." To his growing pile, he also added a AAA membership card and a folded and faded fifty that he kept tucked away in case of emergencies.

In the last slot left to be searched was a wallet-sized photograph of Ava. Not a current picture, but one from her newborn session that Carrie insisted on having a few weeks after her birth. The edges were frayed, a small crease ran along the bottom. Baby Ava lay asleep with her tiny hands tucked under her head, legs folded up to her abdomen, diapered bottom propped. Pete bit his lip hard because he didn't want to break down even though he figured Denna wouldn't care or blame him if he did. He returned the picture of his daughter to the slot in his wallet and tucked the wallet back into his pocket.

He took a cleansing breath that was more a transition than actually voiding the cocktail of confusion and sadness and despair that infected him. "All right, so, what do we do with our time left?"

Denna took a similar breath of her own that also seemed more in-line with transition than dwelling on the despondency of their predicament. "Well, I do have one idea."

The little bit of liveliness that returned to her green gaze and the mischievous bent to her suggestive timbre stirred within Pete a rousing inspiration. "Yeah?"

9:22 p.m.

"This was a great idea," said Pete, feeling loosened up after cracking the cap off yet another Sam Adams Summer Ale. He was relaxed in the Adirondack chair, both feet up on the matching ottoman. He and Denna had dragged both chairs and their footrests from the soft soil at the lakeside area at the bottom of the yard out onto the small dock after filling two coolers with all that remained of the alcoholic beverages and carting them along with a few snacks in tow. Pete had a stash set next to his chair within reach, and Denna had hers.

Though they could barely make each other out as silhouettes in the paling moonlit lake after the sensor light quit, Denna saluted her friend with a sweaty can. "Figured there was no reason to let all of these go to waste."

They drank. And drank some more. Flies and gnats and other unseen tinning insects circled near, drawn by their sweat, blood, and the fruity sweetness of Denna's beverages.

Guards down, no one left in the world to impress, no shame to hold on to and maintain, the two of them let it rip with belly-soothing burps that skipped across the quiet water and echoed in the void. The more alcohol indulged, the louder they bellowed with unbridled laughter. In place of the crying loons, the chirping crickets, and the hooting owls that had been silenced through the passage of daytime into night hours (and the phenomenon also affecting them as well), Echo Lake and its surrounding woodland were serenaded only by the gas expulsions and echoing giggles of the two inebriated.

That lightened mood tamped down, a sobering effect dissipating their buzz when Denna waited for their latest round of cackling to taper.

"The others," she said. Pete settled quiet, placing his half-empty bottle down on the wide armrest of the chair, awaiting the comment or question to follow while the sparks in his head fizzed out. "Where do you think they are? Are they...are they dead?"

Contemplating, Pete slithered his tongue side to side over his bottom lip, looking out to the pale glimmer on the water. "I don't know." He took a plug from the summer ale, let the cool, crisp citrus and tang swish around from cheek to cheek and between his teeth like musky mouthwash, foaming and then swallowing. "I like to believe they're somewhere. Somewhere where they're okay."

"Guess we'll find out for ourselves soon enough, huh?"

She couldn't see it, but Pete nodded. "Yeah. I guess so."

He finished the bottle in two long swills, contemplated opening another, forming a pincer hook with his fingers around the new bottle's sweating neck and lifting it inches out of the cooler, but felt that want slide away. The alcohol clouding his head was no longer accompanied by a good feeling. The worries and doom and gloom couldn't be numbed by indulgence any longer. He released the bottle back to clink and rejoin the few others that were left.

Pete asked, "There's not something we're overlooking here, right? A way out of this that maybe we're not seeing?"

By this point, Denna had also stopped drinking. She let what remained in the last open can continue to sit unconsumed, warming up to air temperature, its bubbliness going flat. Bugs landed on the rim to inspect and taste the backwash. "Unless maybe we could fly out of here, I don't think so."

Under the veil of dry sarcasm, Pete commented with a scoff, "For some reason, I don't think any of these people here have a helicopter."

"Probably would end the same way as driving out of here."

"Or walking."

Denna copied him, exhausting the last of their possible options. "Or walking."

Confirming that final admittance of defeat and having to acquiesce to their inescapable predicament, helpless and forsaken to what would come at some unknown time, gave a squirrely twinge of uneasiness, a sour tremor across Denna's stomach. A touch of bile entered her throat and burned with a fizz. She squeezed her eyes shut, head beginning to twirl, listening intently to her breathing and her heart going wild in her chest to ward off the spell of growing nausea.

"We'd have to be, like, pulled out of here or something." Pete yawned, ending his hypothesis. The chair under him creaked from his limbs stretching out. "What do you think this thing is? Where did it even come from? Is it…I don't know, some weird kind of climate change thing? Did we create it? Some new government lab shit?"

Denna could only utter, "Don't know," and it barely felt like those words eked out with any sense of coherence. She swallowed, eyes still shut, throat still catching fire like a stricken match. Counting seconds after each swallow, much like a potent thunderstorm moving off to the east, she noticed the nausea began to wane as the time she kept track of in low-level whispers increased. Her head was still light, stomach airy, and she wondered if the onset nauseousness had come from her binging. She knocked the remnant can off the armrest to land and roll on the dock. Caught in the gap between boards, the clear, alcoholic seltzer spilled out in foaming dribbles.

Not the way to go, she thought.

This kind of behavior was not her. She was better than this. There was no pride in throwing in the towel and drinking herself into a stupor with the goal of feeling nothing at the end.

"You okay?" Pete said. He sounded barely awake, hardly coherent himself.

Denna rubbed and slapped her face awake, mussing her hair, scratching her scalp. Angry, regretful tears sprouted.

"There was so much more I wanted to do. So much." Each respiration became faster, heavier, deeper, hitching to where Denna was on the verge of hyperventilating. In the pitch-black behind her clenched eyes, a starburst of colors and sensations exploded as her mind raced.

I wanted to be a mother.
I wanted to have that life, being a parent.
I wanted to travel and go places.
So many things I wanted to do.

Spiraling, Denna relinquished the defenses of her struggle to the pull of her overloaded emotions. She wept, stomach beginning to turn, saliva increasing, mucus lining her throat, and exhausted every pent-up frustration, pitching forward and dropping to her knees off the chair and onto the rough planks of the dock. Into the lake she vomited. Two shorter, but just as scorching and sour and violent streams gave chase. She was left reduced to her knees, angled toward the water, long webs of drool hanging and wiggling from her gaped lips. Denna alternated between gasps and hacking out the last globs of poison and mucus. In a short time, her breathing resumed its normal functions and rhythm once the demon of her panic over powerlessness was exorcized. She reconfigured on the dock to sit on her bottom, leaning her back against the footstool and hanging her head toward her lap. She was spent.

"I'm sorry." She spat after using her teeth to scrape off the last of a sour taste still pasted on her tongue. For levity, she added, "I bet now I'm not much for you to look at."

She was surprised not to hear a witty response.

"I'm sorry, that wasn't cool of me to say. I shouldn't've..."

Pete remained silent.

"You know..." In her now more cognizant (and less nauseous) moment, embarrassment warmed her face. There was no reason to say what had come to mind, except now that she'd gotten sick in front of Pete, and her damp skin was cooling in the night air off the lake, there was an awakening and a selfish wish on her part, to be transparent, to be free, and to have more control and author a more positive denouement than life was about to afford either of them. Confirmed by her husband in a fit that was not becoming on him as a person, the intuition Denna had for years had turned out to be right. Because didn't women always know?

"You know...I knew. I knew how you felt about me. Want to know how I knew?"

Pete didn't answer.

Shit. He's probably embarrassed.

"You never touched me."

The little hairs on her arms tickled as they stood.

"It was the last time we all saw each other. When Ava was born and we came to the hospital to meet her and congratulate you guys, Teddy gave you a big hug, kissed Carrie on the cheek…she was so exhausted… I mean, of course she would be. I gave Carrie a hug. When I got to you, you just smiled and kinda did this thing with your hands like…like you just weren't comfortable in your own clothes. You tugged at the neck on your shirt, did the same to your sleeves, and said something about how they keep it so warm in the maternity rooms.

"Ben and Kelsey came in about twenty minutes later, and I watched you hug both of them. That's when I knew. And you know what? It's okay. It's okay."

Her stomach settled. The night was quiet.

Pete remained silent.

Probably passed out, she thought. He had sounded slurry and dozy before. She understood, given the amount of alcohol consumed and strain they'd been under, and didn't want to disturb him. *Probably didn't hear a word of it.*

Denna pulled herself up and into the Adirondack chair, her back conforming to its gently sloped shape, now feeling sleepy herself after all that exertion.

Curiosity niggled at her brain. She turned on the flashlight on her phone, squinting against its brightness, and angled it up slightly, keeping the direct aim of the light low, raising it just enough so the fringes of the beam offered illuminance to the chair beside her on the small dock. While not unexpected, she was still surprised—a lump of grief swelling inside her chest—to find the other chair was empty.

Denna kept the light on, staring at that abandoned space that was now just the bones of the Adirondack chair. The pangs of sorrow and loneliness beat in time with her heart over being the last, over never asking Pete about the things he still wished to do in his life while he was still awake. She hoped he didn't have many regrets and found peace before the end. Maybe even heard a little bit of her confession. Even better (if there was any good in all of this), she hoped he had indeed been asleep when he was taken.

Before she cut the light on her phone, somewhere not too far away, a frog ribbited. Denna shined the flashlight around the banks but couldn't locate the origin amongst the tall weeds.

Left to her fate, Denna switched off her flashlight and curled up in the chair, listening to the gentle wind come on high in the trees, listening to the water softly lap at the pylons of the dock. Listening for the frog again, which occasionally croaked and reminded her it was around. She didn't think she could or would fall asleep until she did, comforted by the hope that when it happened, perhaps she, too, would be asleep and unaware.

September 5
7:03 a.m.

It wasn't until she felt the warmth on her face, could sense the strong presence of light pressing on her shuttered eyelids, and heard the heavy droning of some fat insect bobbing and weaving in a series of crude pathways around her head that Denna realized she was still present. Still here. She made it to the morning. Not yet ready to move a muscle as she was adjusting to the realization of her continued existence (which, much as she would have preferred to have gone unaware in her sleep, this surprise was in no way a disappointment), she took a grateful breath of the clean and thin, though pre-autumnally nippy, lake air through her nose and yawned to clear out her waking lungs. She opened her eyes to squint against piercing glints and glimmers refracting on the lake bed surrounding her peninsula. The cutting buzz and shadow of a curious dragonfly crossed every which way in her orbit but kept a respectful distance over the sunlit dock.

She sat up in the Adirondack chair before doing a thorough systems check and nearly regretted her impulsion. The hangover was weak, but enough to feel like every action she performed was being done in bullet time, out of sync with everything else in her snow globe at Echo Lake moving at normal speed. Thoughts banged around of how thankful she felt, but also didn't feel. Behind her eyes a pressure became evident when she rubbed the tendrils of sleep and the fog of blurriness away. The headache had finally come. Was that what woke her? How long had she had it?

Won't be much longer now.

"So be it," she said, feeling a little dumb for talking aloud to herself, although there was no one else around to hear it. She had grown tired of being a victim to the waiting game. She became numb to the fear of her hourglass being almost empty. Maybe this onset of bravery came in tandem with the start of a new day, as things to dread always seem less frightening in the optimism of fresh and powerful sunlight versus the nihilism that grows in the dark, but she was no longer afraid. She was more impatient. She just wanted it over already.

But not before a final task to complete.

Denna checked her phone because that action was ingrained. No signal.

The baseline nausea remained with her, churning within her gut like a shaken soda bottle when she rose to her feet. Denna sighed then promptly sank to her knees at the edge of the dock and puked into the lake for a second time. In the disorientation of weaving past the ottomans and chairs she and Pete brought onto the dock the previous night, Denna knew she had to eat something. The waves of dizziness combined with the notion of food filling her unsettled stomach set her off again and she hosed down the dock with the last bits of Chex Mix, alcohol, and bile at her sandaled feet.

"Ugh. So gross."

Hunched in that spot, supporting herself with hands on knees, she gasped and drooled out strings of spit that clung to her bottom lip until her empty stomach settled and the spell of dry heaving abated. All she had to drink the night before that had seemed like a good idea at the time had become something to lament. Though, swearing never to do it again was no longer a worry.

Uncertain if the throbbing in her head was a symptom of a hangover or the strange force inhabiting Echo Lake having its effect on her, Denna moseyed onward, feet shuffling, stomach swaying, up to the lake house. Clutching the walls to get in, she made it to the bathroom where she relieved what felt like about a gallon's worth of pee from her body and then threw up in the sink.

"Jesus," she said after running the sink and rinsing out her mouth. "I've really got to stop drinking."

There wasn't much in the way of food once her stomach felt ready to handle some intake. The salads and fruit had been tossed the night before, and most of the snacks were hauled out to the dock by her and Pete. Denna would have preferred bread to make some toast or to find a sleeve of plain crackers in the cupboards, but neither of those options were available. There were some leftover burger rolls but no toaster, and she was still feeling picky enough to not eat them plain or turn on the small oven. Instead, she settled on an open bag of plain tortilla chips that had started to go stale and filled a glass with tepid water at the sink.

"Fucking breakfast of champions."

She remembered then that none of them had intended to bring breakfast food (or even fixtures for coffee) for the morning because they'd planned to drive to a diner called Bonnie's in the nearby town of Woodstock before going on their separate ways back to Serling Oaks and returning to the busy lives and family that awaited them there. For Denna it would have just been her and Teddy, whereas the others had kiddos to greet them. Family errands to run. Lawns to mow, maybe. Classrooms to finish setting up, certainly, between herself, Carrie, and Kelsey.

Those rooms wouldn't get done. Wouldn't be ready.

They would never see their students. Their students may never know what happened to their teachers who had disappeared and never came to school.

These thoughts led down a rabbit hole of more nevers she wouldn't experience again.

Jeez, she thought with an incredulous shake of her head, surfacing from the well of shitty thoughts. *Those plans of going together to breakfast and then home felt like they were conceived forever ago.*

"How quickly everything changes."

Snacking on pliable, brittle chips, with whatever crumbs that fell wayside from her mouth left to litter the floor, Denna brought the bag and her water to the coffee table where she came upon her list and the pen used to write it.

Kneeling down beside the table, Denna uncapped the pen and added the fifth name to those amongst the missing.

Pete Turnbull

Her epitaph, which didn't require much thought: *A very kind soul*

Last on the list, it was time for her to add herself, *Denna Meers*, and she found she didn't have a hard time forming the curvatures of the connected letters as she had struggled when documenting her husband's name.

Her hand was steady now because her mind was coming to ease. But a memorial statement didn't readily pop to mind. Her attempts of consideration (anything that wasn't pretentious or silly) were interrupted by a sound she thought she heard out front.

"Was that a door?"

Denna scrambled up to see.

7:23 a.m.

To Denna's alarm, looking out the window, she confirmed that sound had been a door all right.

"Oh no. Nooo…"

The shut door belonged to a Dodge Charger decorated in the standard navy blue with yellow stripes along the side panels with designations associated with the New York State Trooper fleet. The single patrol vehicle was parked out on the long grass with the trooper herself approaching on the cobbled stone walk in her crisp gray uniform and hair tucked up into the sharp tan Stetson that sat at a perfect zero-degree angle. Behind darkened sunglasses that obscured her eyes, the officer made subtle turns of her head, inspecting the grounds during her casual but confident procession. She was saddled with all kinds of equipment on her belt within close reach, keeping her right hand gripped to her radio while the left swung as a tight pendulum in accordance with her steps.

"No, no, no." Denna rushed to the front door, pulling it open to step out, surprising the officer, who froze on the walk, free hand going right to the butt of her service weapon, thumb ready to unsnap the locking flap that kept the weapon in its holster. The hand that had been on the radio went up in a proactive, defensive "wait" gesture.

"Hold it right there, ma'am."

"Officer, you can't be here—"

"Just take it easy and listen to me."

"But you don—"

The officer reiterated with her hand that was up and lifted her chin, indicating she needed to be heard and listened to, maintaining calm and authority through an even, almost singsongy but firm timbre that underscored her instructions—asking but not really asking. "Just listen to me first, ma'am, okay? Can you do that?"

Difficult as it was, Denna had to accept it was already too late. She couldn't help the officer now. Her posture slouched where she stood in the doorway, reining in everything wanting to deluge from her mouth to grant the officer her chance to speak. "Yes."

"Okay." The trooper relaxed her stance but kept her distance. She dropped her lifted hand and removed the other from the butt end of her service weapon. With slow, deliberate movements, she removed her sunglasses and tucked them into a pocket on her belt, stripping away a layer that obscured her humanity beneath the uniform, revealing friendly hazel eyes to help establish a connection and deter confrontation. "I'm Officer Lewis. I'm here looking for a Pete or Peter Turnbull. Do you know him?"

Denna reminded herself to just answer simply. A congestion of emotion built in her throat, tears warming her eyes. "Yes."

"Is he inside?"

Denna shook her head, those tears brimming.

"My department received a call this morning from his sister. She was worried about him because of a message he left her last night. She's been trying to get ahold of him, but he's not answering his phone."

Denna had forgotten about Pete calling his sister Becky, hoping he had gotten through when she didn't pick up. "She got his message?"

"On my way here I saw a Jeep off the road mangled into a tree. I stopped and checked it out. Looks like whoever was inside left the scene, and it hasn't been reported. Do you know anything about that accident?"

A single tear escaped and ran. Denna leaned into the doorframe.

"My husband. He was trying to leave."

Officer Lewis blinked, keeping a poker face. "What's your name?"

"Denna." She wiped away the trail of her fallen tear. "Denna Meers."

"Denna. My name is Sarah. Is there anyone else inside the house with you?"

Tears fell freely now. Denna shook her head because words couldn't push through the restriction of her tightening throat. The yearning to tell everything, how she had lost Ben and Carrie and Pete and Kelsey and Teddy (her heart winced in grief at her thought of him), overwhelmed every cell of her being. She could hardly hold herself upright.

"Denna." This time when Officer Lewis said her name, there was a slight trip, a stumble, a tremble in her voice, exposing an uneasiness not typical with veterans of law enforcement more in control of their emotions in stressful situations. Denna wondered if Sarah Lewis was a rookie, or relatively new to the uniform. Denna thought the woman trooper had a youthful appearance now that the sunglasses had been removed, but looks often deceived experience. She didn't want to make that assumption. Officer Lewis repeated her name with a bit more confidence. "Denna. I need to know: are you in danger?"

There was no use lying even though the truth was beyond belief. Denna nodded.

"I think you need to come with me." Officer Lewis relieved the hand on her walkie and held it out, welcoming, inviting Denna toward her.

Through her light, quivering sobs, which expelled all the energy she had, Denna managed, "Where?"

"To the station. Just a few miles away. I'll get your statement there, and we—"

"No. No, you don't understand—"

"I think it would be easier for you not to re—"

"No, you're not listening to me—"

"Denna, I think it would be in your best—"

Denna forwent crying and put every ounce of energy into her voice. "YOU'RE NOT LISTENING!"

Officer Lewis's face tightened as the echo of Denna's words banged off the exterior walls of the house and the crowd of surrounding trees. She refrained from speaking, showing her willingness to now hear Denna out, still trying to keep the peace.

"We can't leave. It won't let us go."

There was little patience left in Lewis's voice. "What won't?"

Denna looked around as if there was something unusual to see in their ordinary setting. "I don't know what it is, but it's been taking everyone. Teddy and Pete…they tried to get out, but it kept them here."

Lewis played along with the narrative, that poker face not telling which side of the fence her faith landed in this story. "So you're saying we can't drive out of here?"

Denna confirmed.

"Okay. Now let me tell you why we have to leave, Denna. When I pulled off the road to inspect the accident I saw, I tried to report it to dispatch. I couldn't raise them on my radio or from my car. I tried again when I pulled up here because that's my protocol—to let them know I've arrived."

"There's no signal out here."

"That seems to be the case." Lewis kept that congenial agreement between them. "Usually, my equipment has a pretty good boost for areas just like this, but yes, you're right, for some reason I'm not getting a signal. You're saying something is keeping you here? I can help you. Let me help you."

"I can't."

"Come with me."

Denna resumed her refusals, sliding down the doorframe now to sit in the open area of the threshold.

For the first time during their conversation, Officer Lewis took a step forward. It was a cautious step, but one that began to close the gap. She removed her hat, revealing more of her true self, displaying a matted and sweaty dome of pinned-up, strawberry-tinted hair. "Can I ask you what happened to the others?"

Again, Denna found no reason to be coy about the facts.

"They got these terrible headaches, and then…they just vanished."

"And you're telling me that will happen if we stay?"

Denna confirmed.

"Then don't we owe it to everyone who was here and anyone else who could come here to try and leave?"

Denna couldn't tell if Officer Lewis believed any of what she was saying (ha, who would?) or if she was just doing her job and trying to be calming and coaxing without raising any sort of confrontation if she could help it. Denna knew how this looked to an outsider such as a police officer—people were missing, which meant a probable crime took place, and it was their job to start putting the pieces together while keeping everyone safe. Denna was the last member of her group with five adults now unaccounted for. Surely, she was a suspect of some kind. She was the only one with a story that had any number of answers. To the officer's credit, she was good at her job, and that hint of having the jitters had been contained. Lewis was now making a passionate plea.

"I can tell you, Denna, with absolute certainty, that if dispatch doesn't hear back from me within a certain window of time, they'll send more officers to look for me. They'll send them here. If something is here harming everyone, we need to keep them and everyone else out. We need to help them."

Denna was certain this strategy was all part of Officer Lewis's training. Gain the confidence of the suspect (not that she was an official suspect yet… at least she didn't think she was) through amicable, encouraging, examining, even guiding dialogue, while trying to avoid opinions on her behalf and strict disagreement that would lead to conflict, but also remaining sturdy in the position of being a law enforcer and protector, thus having to consider the safety of all others present and not.

She's probably also spooked as all fuck and wants to get outta here.

Officer Lewis completed closing the gap, crouching down at the foot of the short steps in front of Denna, keeping that inviting hand extended. "Come with me, Denna."

If the officer was afraid or even reluctant of the unknown surrounding them, she succeeded in stowing it away. Her confidence, perhaps driven by the badge and uniform she wore, had penetrated and the strength in her unflinching hazel stare was motivating. She was thinking of those outside the perimeter. Those who could become trapped like them.

The pressure in her head withstanding, Denna figured what the hell. She had been prepared for her ending anyway and hadn't expected to wake up this morning, so everything from the gorgeous sunlight on her face to the hovering dragonfly, fresh air, and the extra minutes to experience the beauty of the world and complete the unfinished tasks on her ledger was all on bonus time. For that she was appreciative.

Except for the vomiting and skull throbbing. She could have done without any of that.

But beggars couldn't be choosers.

"Come on, Denna."

Hand still out there between them.

Denna reached out and accepted.

7:32 a.m.

"Protocols are protocols, unfortunately. You'll have to ride in the back."

For someone as harmless and goody-two-shoes as Denna had been her entire life, it felt like a cruel joke that her existence on this earth was about to come to its end while stashed in the back of a police cruiser.

But, again, there's that thing about being a beggar.

To her comfort, at least, the handcuffs weren't applied. So there was that anyway.

With added potency, Officer Lewis shut the reinforced door then climbed into the front. She tossed her hat onto the passenger seat, tapped down any unruly wisps of her strawberry-red hair that was pinned up along the sides of her head, then checked and typed on an open laptop sitting on a swivel tray coming off the center console while Denna inspected the bareness of her cramped surroundings. Both back seat windows contained guards that resembled window blinds except made of steel, and true to every cop drama she'd ever seen on television, the doors were missing their latches to be opened from the inside. A clear, thick partition divided the front and back seats, with only a series of small holes drilled along the top to allow airflow and communication between.

"Dispatch, this is Five-Eight-One, come back?"

While buckling her belt, Lewis spoke into the remote receiver of her vehicle's radio. Dropped and shook her head when no response was returned.

"Dispatch. This is Five. Eight. One. Confirm?"

She sighed, hung up the receiver. Lewis looked into the rearview mirror to find Denna checking out the back. "Been the same thing since I got out here. No reception." Then, to herself: "Hopefully, when we get out of here…"

Softly, Denna scoffed, not ready to buy into that faith.

As Lewis put the car in Reverse and started rolling back onto Bass Lane, Denna took one last sweeping look at the L-shaped, ranch-style lake house and its patchwork of numerous facades, which gave the small home a quirky quaintness that played an unassuming contrast to the unseen, malicious force at work out here. It was impossible to adequately reflect on the last twelve hours or so, but also unavoidable not to try. Her mind was a dense fog of fraught exhaustion, so many frailties, so many emotions, and goddamn her head hurt so much, and her stomach sat uneasy. She glanced at Pete and Carrie's Mazda parked next to them and Ben and Kelsey's 4Runner out front that would continue to be ornaments—devastating testaments to her friends—sitting undisturbed on the overgrown lawn for who knew how long. There was also the abandoned push mower standing yards away from the red panel van belonging to the missing homeowner—her friend, John—that had been parked on the property since before she and the others arrived. Mixed feelings of hot and cold flowed through her veins and through her thoughts. She was sad for her lost friends, happy for herself, thankful for the chance to escape, and also anxious, worried, and unsure how she and Officer Lewis were going to get out, if they even could. But Denna Meers didn't have an opportunity to wade around in the loss of her friends, her hopes, her uncertainties, or her attachments to this ill-fated place. The cruiser shifted gears and they pulled away.

Denna took a sharp, preparatory inhale as a swimmer would just before plunging beneath the surface.

"It'll be all right," said Lewis, who perhaps sensed or even spotted in the rearview all of Denna's anxieties that were surely overtly displayed on her face and in her fidgeting.

Already stricken with a headache—whether or not it was *the* headache remained to be determined—there came a soft, pitchy whine like a dentist's drill that settled deep in Denna's ears not long into their departure. She cleared her throat, stretched and flexed her jaw, and furiously wiggled a finger against the outer ridges of both ears in hopes to pop her ears and alleviate the sound.

"You doing okay back there?" said Lewis.

"Can't you feel it?"

That low-end drilling increased. Flashes of sunlight through the trees and then shadows of branches rolled over the cruiser's windshield, at times spotlighting the specks of dead bugs and grime. Attuned but unfocused in her sensitivities, Denna could hear each whoosh of those passing ribbons of light and shadow. The muted hum of the car's engine faded away. The rumbling of the wheels over the cracked and crumbling road turned muffled, hollow. That piercing white whine remained constant, though, growing. The drilling wasn't just in her ears now; it migrated to the fillings in her teeth, into the core behind the walls of her throat, latching on to the stem of her brain at the pivot where her neck met the base of her skull, casting waves of tinnitus throughout her head, ringing in her teeth.

Then came the shock waves of pain that pulsed out of the center of her head.

She cried out. With fingertips of short but cutting nails, she dug deep into her folding brow that showcased all of its trenches, and she gripped all around her scalp, desperate to mitigate the squeezing ache. She hoped to numb the agony put upon her by creating her own through the application and sinking of her nails into the flesh around her skull.

"Denna?"

Officer Lewis scanned her rearview then shot a look back over her shoulder.

"Denna? You okay?"

Officer Lewis's words were distorted, echoey, faraway.

Everything seemed to play out in slow motion.

Denna forced open her eyes.

The world through her sight had begun to turn and warp.

Approaching off the road to the right, her and Teddy's Jeep—what she recognized of it—sat dented, scarred with scrapes and scratches, rippled like the best kind of potato chips, and melded to a tree. Shards and pebbles of loose glass glinted and winked at her ominously, each giving off an excruciating flash that seared her eyes through to the back of her head and out the canals of her ears.

Reality sped back up when the cruiser cut a hard shift to the left, centering back on the road. Denna was tossed to her right, banging her shoulder and elbow of the same appendage off the door and partition. "Jesus."

She stopped in her reach to buckle up when she saw Officer Lewis's straight posture against the backing of the front seat had altered to her leaning forward, held by the tightening of her own safety belt but sunk to the right. Lewis's elbow rested on the center console, and her head was dipped. She pressed three fingers against her right-side temple. Her face distorted into a tight, twisted grimace.

"Oh no."

The tires screeched with another hard swerve in Lewis's struggle to stay on the road.

"Officer Lewis!"

Lewis groaned. "Urrrhhhh… What's happening?"

She tugged on the wheel, and the car shifted again, cutting right.

The spidery arms of the trees and the strip of road beyond the windshield turned blurry to Denna, her eyes distorting everything against the crushing pain in her head. She could no longer make out the readings on the gauges, the small text, or even the mechanisms on Lewis's dashboard. Could hardly see Officer Lewis as anything other than a blot of her dark uniform and reddish hair being a foot ahead of Denna on the other side of the barrier. Everything morphing into a stomach-turning haze in the wake of unrelenting, unbearable suffering.

Momentum changed. What Denna couldn't see, she sensed after being shot forward into the clear partition. The seat and car beneath her hiccuped, lurched, then began to drift without the push of the engine. They were slowing. Lewis had slipped her foot off the gas and was jostling the brake.

Both women exhaled hisses and cries of pain as the cruiser rolled to a slowing stop nearing the shoulder of Bass Lane. Officer Lewis had enough effort in her to throw the transmission into Park to keep them from creeping over the edge of the road and rolling off into the woods.

Denna ground the side of her head hard against the barrier, finding a modicum of waning pain in that applied pressure that left smears of the oils on her skin. It seemed Lewis was trying an act similar, pitched forward, laying her forehead against the hard curvature of the steering wheel.

"What is this?" Lewis gritted out.

Denna kept grinding away, smudging, streaking, rolling her head sideways and back along the partition. "I told you… I told you…"

She sunk almost every top row tooth into her bottom lip, hard enough that when she slackened the pressure and withdrew, there was the faint, warm taste of coins with a pasty stickiness ringing the bottom half around her mouth.

"He was so right." Denna thought of Pete. How solemn and dour and defeated he had been coming back to the lake house the previous night. He managed to get far enough to the outer rim of this unknown phenomenon to get a message out to his sister. It found its way through the cracks, but he couldn't proceed any farther then, and they wouldn't be able to now. The barrier of this alien force would keep them. Take them. "We can't get out."

Lewis hissed out a long, throaty, gurgling trail of anguish that crescendoed with a scream.

"We can't get out. We can't get out." Denna repeated this pessimistic, rhythmic mantra that ebbed and flowed in calm, fluttering whispers.

"We can't get out."

A breath.

"Can't get out."

A breath.

She pressed the center of her forehead against the barrier, eyes closed.

"We can't…"

A breath.

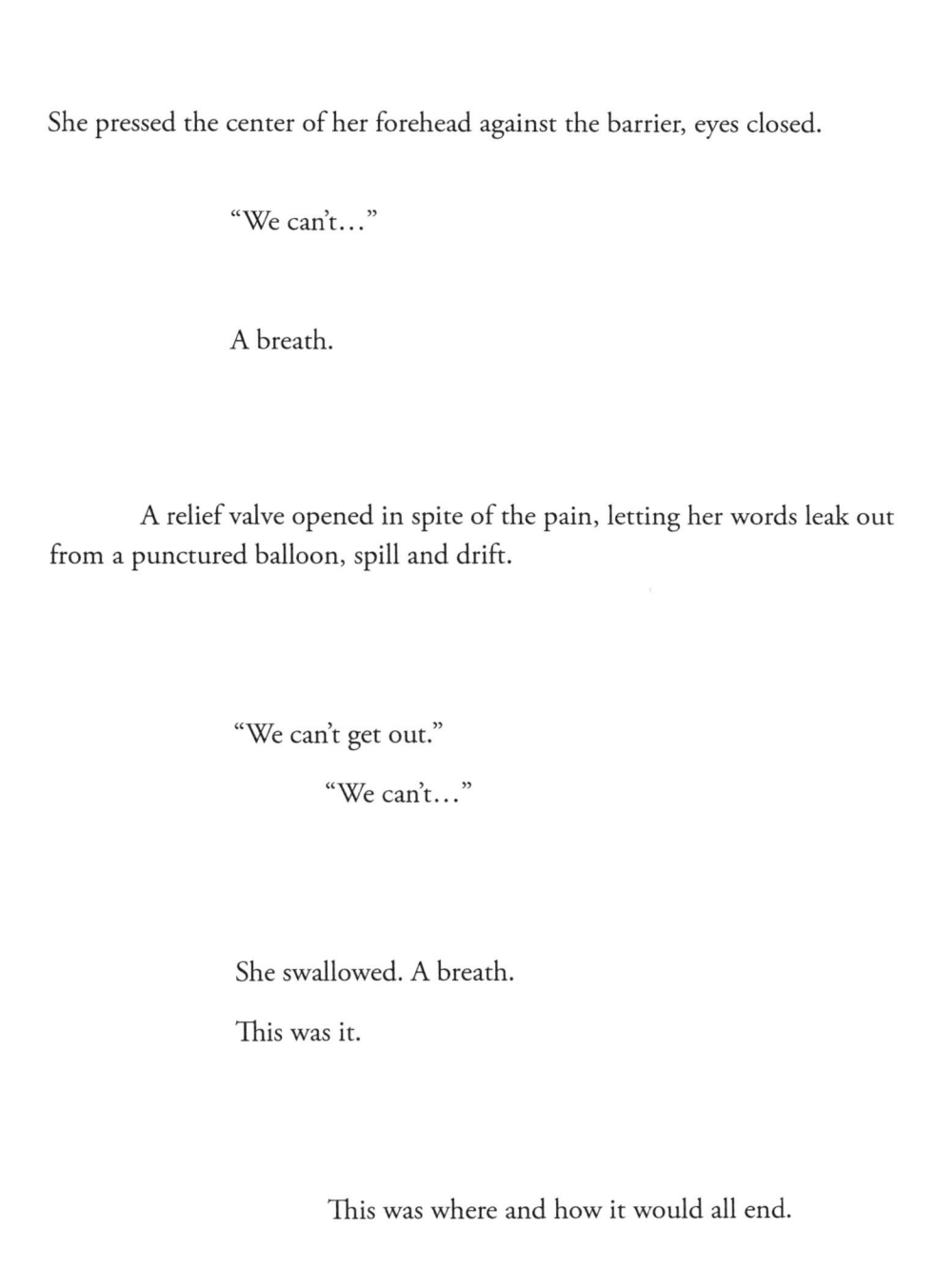

A relief valve opened in spite of the pain, letting her words leak out from a punctured balloon, spill and drift.

"We can't get out."

"We can't…"

She swallowed. A breath.

This was it.

This was where and how it would all end.

"We can't… He was right."

She would just keep talking, she decided. Hearing herself and not the droning whine of diverging pain.

Keep talking. Breathing. Talking herself to sleep.

"We can't get out. No." They had exhausted all options. They had tried everything.
"Not unless we're pulled or take—"

Denna paused. Held her breath.

Her thoughts searched within the short string of those words.

Eyes fluttered open. Breath spreading fog after fog onto the partition.

Words uttered by Pete.

"Pulled. Or taken."

She repeated those words, making a connection.

"Pulled or taken…"

Again and again.

Over and over.

"Pulled or taken."

Something there.
She tried to latch on to it.

"Pulled or taken."

It was right there. Two separate live wires. She kept speaking.

"Pulled or taken. Pulled or taken."

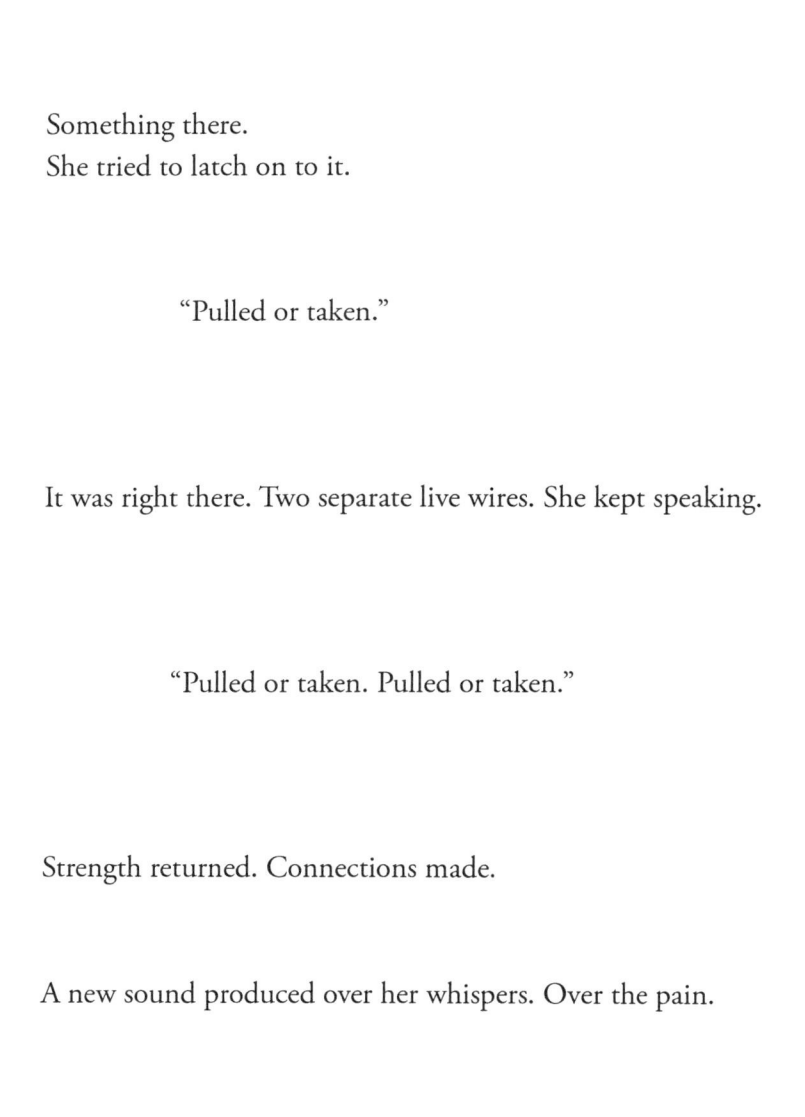

Strength returned. Connections made.

A new sound produced over her whispers. Over the pain.

Heartbeat.

"Sarah."

In her ears: *whump, whump*

"Sarah."

Faster and faster: *whump, whump, whump*

Building. Overpowering.

A push to save them all.

"SARAH LEWIS!"

Officer Lewis rose from her slump over the wheel. Picked herself up.

"You've got to listen to me, Sarah."

Sarah collapsed back against her seat. Groaned. Denna was pressed to the barrier right behind her. Mere inches of transparent panel separated them. Though Sarah was merely a blur, Denna could see that her shape was moving, fighting.

"You've got to drive, Sarah. Drive." Denna swore with all her conviction, "I can get us out."

Moaning through her anguish, Officer Lewis bore through each breath. "You can do it, Sarah."

Lewis acknowledged by grasping on to the steering wheel with her left hand. With her right, she gripped the shift column. Denna could barely see this, but listened to the officer's every move, her every grunt. Her desire to withstand. To persist.

"Drive."

A series of tugs on the column to get the arm to budge. The vehicle clunked and rocked into another gear (Denna visualized this being Reverse). Clunked again bypassing another (Neutral). Then a third time (Drive).

"Go, Sarah. Go."

Lewis wailed unabated as she struck the gas pedal with a clumsy lead foot. The cruiser's tires peeled, screaming on the rough pavement. The car launched forward. The sudden kick from inertia pitched Denna back into the seat like a rag doll where she splayed. The car jerked left, followed by hard swerves this way and that to aim down the center of the lane. Denna couldn't see, didn't bother trying to focus, but trusted wholeheartedly that Lewis would keep them on the road.

The engine revved with a droning that flooded the cabin space. Denna felt the force of acceleration pressing her back into the seat. The grip around her head tightened. She blindly reached her right hand along the top corner of the seat backing and found the latch for her seat belt. With her left hand, she felt around the space next to her hip to locate the buckle. She got both.

The time came for the most crucial direction.

"Sarah… Put…put on the cruise control!"

Denna repeated this demand, vision still so hazy that she kept her eyes shut to ward off the ugly grumblings in her gut, kept shouting her instruction until Officer Lewis confirmed. It was a relief to hear Sarah's voice over all the ringing noise and all the pressure. Still coherent. Still with that determination.

All that was left was Sarah steering them, keeping them on the road.

And to hope. Pray.

The car would do the rest. The car wouldn't be deterred by pain. It would go on its own, programmed, taking them onward, but still needing to be guided.

They just needed to hold out. Stay awake.

Denna brought the belt across her folded abdomen and lap and snapped the latch home.

She kept singing praises, encouraging Sarah.

She kept praying.

The world slowed down again.

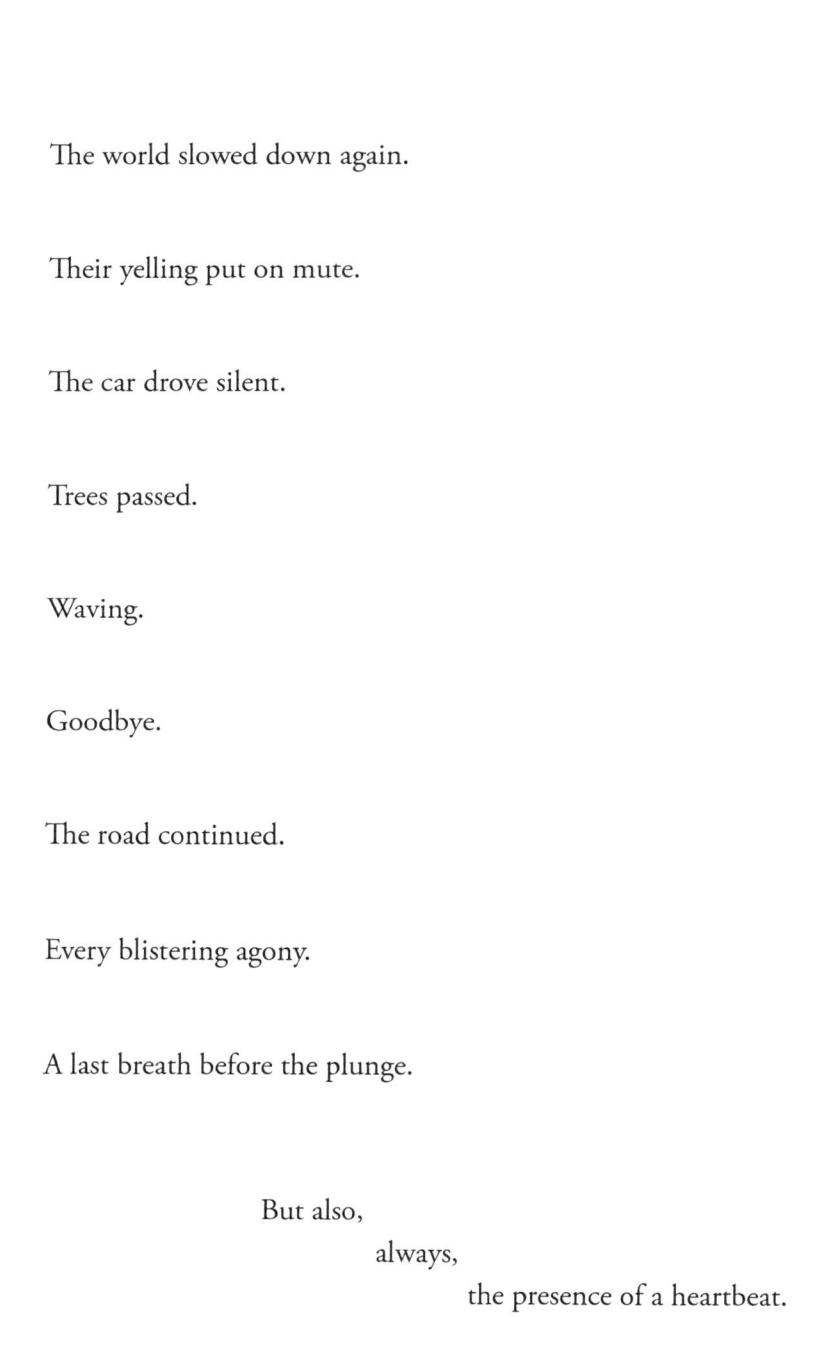

Their yelling put on mute.

The car drove silent.

Trees passed.

Waving.

Goodbye.

The road continued.

Every blistering agony.

A last breath before the plunge.

        But also,
            always,
                the presence of a heartbeat.

The archway of trees passed, becoming in their wake.

Brilliant, unfiltered sunlight lovingly enveloped them.

The pain lifted. A mist burning off.

Denna's sight returned. She gasped just in time to see Bass Lane come to its end, meeting the junction of Route 33 outside of Echo Lake.

But they were going too fast.

"Sarah!"

She barely cried out before the police cruiser skipped over the perpendicular lanes as if the vehicle weighed no more than a stone as it bounced across a bed of water. Officer Lewis's body herked and jerked loosely around, belted in—

Passed out, Denna had been able to think last moment.

—before they careened off the other side, becoming momentarily weightless in flight and smashing through a front line of cornstalks in a crop field that went on as an ocean at the bottom of the slope.

The hard impacts sent them topsy-turvy. Glass shattered. Metal dented inward. The landscape of thick green and leafy stalks flipped outside the now open-air windows. Denna's world grayed.

Finally, they settled, right side up. The cruiser landed, the back wheels last to come down home on the earth, but Denna was still catching up to the present. The disorientating residuals of rolling over and over messed with her orientation as the electrical messages in her system began to short out.

Denna saw Officer Lewis slouched forward, held in place by her safety belt. No way to know if Sarah was breathing before Denna's vision once more failed, this time dimming out.

As she was slipping under, through a tunnel came a crackle of static.

Then a distant, impassive voice.

"Car Five-Eight-One, respond?"

-crackle-

"Five-Eight-One?"

-crackle-

"All units…"

3:04 p.m.

The air had a smell to it. Barely there but discernible.

Sanitized.

Nearby vents ran steady with a soothing whisper.

Voices somewhere close by became elevated, animated. Not in a combative way, but in the loose mash-up of turn-taking that was characteristic of a lively discussion. Their volume lowered a few decibels but not their tenacity.

"…you think the government's testing something out there and it went wrong?"

"…how else can you explain…"

"…the sheer implications of such a weapon if it existed—"

"Or spill, if that's what this was."

"We won't know for sure until that area gets thoroughly studied…"

Denna opened her eyes to find herself in the sparse conditions of a hospital room (beige walls with two pieces of artwork depicting seasonal, lush landscapes; signs of routine procedures; and one whiteboard where her name had been written above the name of the attending physician, Dr. Ahmed). She was lying on her back in an elevated bed with the side rails up. The thin white bedsheet had only been brought up to her waist, the rest of her covered in a white-and-blue-checkered patient gown. She noticed quickly when moving her fingers that, along with a green patient wristband featuring a barcode, farther up that same arm she had a single line of clear fluid running intravenously. Scoping around, she saw the bed next to her on the other half of the room was empty and lay flat, still made. The pillow on the inclined end was full and free of wrinkles or head impressions. In the nearest corner by the windows, where the drawn blinds let in muted light that was either late day or early morning, she spied the clothes she had worn, sitting folded on top of the seat of a green leather chair. Standing at the foot of her bed was a lean blond woman in burgundy scrubs, her back to Denna as she looked up at a television, remote in hand. She was adjusting the volume on a news talk show on CNN. The chyron along the bottom of the screen read: **DISASTER AT LAKE IN UPSTATE NY.**

The subheading: **No bodies recovered. Almost two dozen seemingly vanished.**

Denna sat up. Her movement alerted the woman in burgundy to her rousing.

"Oh, hello." The attending nurse adjusted the paper surgical mask covering her nose and mouth. "You've kinda been in and out of it the last few hours. How are you feeling?"

A quick consideration of all exteriors—moving both arms, legs, her neck, back—and Denna was surprised to say she felt fine, great even. A little jittery and she thought she might have sat up too quickly, but the nurse assured her that was normal. She shook her head to make sure, and nope—no headache.

"That's great. Well, I'm Melanie, your nurse for the next couple hours." Nurse Melanie set the remote down on a rolling food tray set next to the bed. "Feel free to change the channel if you want. A bunch of us are caught up with this stuff. Sounds like you were there?"

Taking in part of the current segment, Denna saw in a small picture-in-picture window provided by the program an aerial view of what was identified on-screen as Echo Lake, NY, as it was being discussed by the commentators. From the air, she didn't recognize the area of countryside and a lake until a passing glimpse, which must have been shot with a drone for its smooth intimate sweep low along the top of the trees and over the water, showed briefly a small dock with two Adirondack chairs facing out toward the body of the lake.

"Again," said one of the reporters on the panel, "these are live shots, if you're just joining us. The affected area around the lake has been completely cordoned off. No reporters, not even local emergency services, have been allowed past the border. All reports now are coming from outside the impacted area."

Perimeter shots on the roads surrounding the woods showed an immense presence of parked police vehicles and officers preventing access to the area by stationing a rope of rolling yellow tape on tall landscape markers piercing the grounds. Other images showed orange sawhorses set up, electronic detour signs blinking directions, and cops directing town traffic.

"Right now we are working with local affiliates and agencies to report this story. We'll have live coverage with our own correspondents there, on the ground at Echo Lake just outside the town of Woodstock, New York, this evening starting at six."

The show's host, or who Denna presumed to be host, filled the screen in a medium shot at the round glass-topped table. The middle-aged man with a coif of dark hair graying on the sides, decked in a gray suit and skinny black tie, shuffled his papers and looked directly into the camera.

"As we've been reporting on for the last few hours, a small community in upstate New York has become the focal point of a probable incident. How severe an incident? Well, details are in short supply right now as to the makeup and scale of this possible disaster, but what we do know is this: over a dozen, maybe even closer to twenty people in the vicinity of Echo Lake have gone missing. What began with rescue efforts regarding a wrecked police vehicle just off Route 33 earlier today has beco—"

"Excuse me," Denna said to the nurse. "Do you know anything about Sarah Lewis? She was the officer in the car I was taken out of…"

Nurse Melanie's eyes narrowed in thought. "She's not on my rounds so I really don't know, sorry. But Dr. Ahmed wanted me to tell him when you were awake, and I think he would know more. I'll let him know, okay? Hopefully, he can answer that for you."

After Melanie saw herself out, Denna scooted down, dropping her legs over the front of the bed. The tender bottoms of her feet went chilly on the icy floor. She stood and was hit with spots obscuring her vision as the room teetered off-kilter. Denna gripped on to the IV pole and wheeled it closer, waiting for the bout of dizziness to pass.

"…know there is a reported individual presumed to have gotten out of this situation developing at Echo Lake…"

Denna blinked the last of the spots away, looked up at the television.

"As of right now we don't have a name," said the news agency host, "but we learned this woman was taken to General Hospital in nearby Serling Oaks for observation and for minor injuries sustained in the accident involving a police vehicle…"

No accompanying picture of her showed up on the screen, for which Denna was thankful. No one in her family and very few friends even knew she and Teddy had gone out of town for an overnight, so it would have been quite the shock for all of them to see her face, or hear her name, pop up on national news. Though, she feared, that unfortunate occurrence seemed but a matter of time given the extensive coverage taking precedence over much larger, world-pressing stories that were now reduced to short sentences running along the ticker at the bottom of the screen. Denna knew from reputation how scavenger-like these journalists were—they wouldn't just have her name by the end of the day but also her blood type and what she scored on her SATs.

The room reoriented. Denna brought the IV pole in with her to the bathroom. After flushing and washing her hands, she examined herself in the mirror under an ugly golden-hue light. A good bruise of dark purple with a yellow halo at its base had formed high on her left cheek; one eye was bloodshot. There were a few scrapes, mostly on her arms, a good nick at the ridge of her left ear, but nothing that required anything but maybe a dab from an antiseptic pad. For being in a rollover, she believed she'd fared quite well. Miraculously well, even. Not one broken bone. No stitches. No signs of a concussion.

She hoped Officer Lewis could say the same.

Exiting the bathroom, Denna was no longer alone in her room.

"Ah, good to see you fully awake and up and moving," said the elderly lank man next to her bed. He spoke in a quiet, thick Indian accent that was slightly muffled behind his own surgical mask and stood hunched at a rolling tray of his own that held an open laptop. His silver-infused short mane and the sprigs of meager beard popping out around the edges of his mask added to the distinction in what was visible of his weathered but alert face. His eyes, when on her, became almonds glinting like the overhead lights out in the corridor. He swam in a white coat that looked a size or two too big, baggy, especially around his bony arms and hunched shoulders. He typed something in a labored hunt-and-peck manner while Denna rolled her IV along toward the bed.

"Oh, here, allow me."

Denna thought it hilarious that this slow-moving, frail-looking gentleman closer in age and resemblance to Master Yoda was speeding (or maybe he thought he was speeding) across the tiled floor to her to offer an arm and assistance back to the bed. She accepted, though still clutched harder to the rolling IV pole in the instance the spins returned.

"I am Dr. Ahmed, the attending physician for you. I wanted to stop in and see how you are holding up?"

Denna reached the end of the bed and sat. Definitely felt better after sitting. "Good, mostly. Um. Got a little dizzy getting up. Lightheaded."

"Any nausea, headaches, pains, cramps?"

"Not really. Not right now," Denna said, shaking her head.

"Mm-hmm."

"Feeling much better now than when I was out there." With a jut of her chin, Denna indicated the television where coverage continued about the happenings in and around Echo Lake. Ahmed gave a cursory glance up at the screen, almost not even interested or concerned.

"Yes, well, that's good to hear," he said. "Certainly, the lightheadedness, the dizziness, headaches, nausea—that's all fairly common with your condition."

"My condition?"

"Your pregnancy."

Everything after that Denna didn't hear in full. Something about blood tests and an EKG and the results of a brain trauma test (in the paperwork given to her later she read those tests came back fine). Then something about her primary doctor's office (they were contacted for a follow-up in the next week), about being discharged in the morning (this following one more night of observation), and about how they'll continue with IV saline (simply to maintain hydration). Throughout the explanations, Denna slipped into a different stream of consciousness where the already suppressed volume of Dr. Ahmed competed with a soft drumming in her ears that she attributed to a heartbeat, whether it was her own—

She came back around when asked if she had any questions.

"Oh. Um." The branching lines of thought across her mind came together, converging on a single infatuation.

"Pregnancy."

That word felt weird, alien on her tongue. She repeated it. Didn't feel like a word at all, more like some concoction of gibberish she made up. Yet, that gobbledygook carried all the weight of immediacy in the world.

"The baby." That sounded even stranger coming out of her mouth, inflecting more like a question. "The baby's…okay?"

"Baby is just fine," said Ahmed. He expressed a smile that revealed itself in the squinting of his eyes. His voice was still quiet and gentle and reaffirming. "No worries."

"I was…" Denna about laughed. Everything before now, the life she'd lived, the choices she'd made, felt so forever ago. "I have been on the pill. How am I pregnant?"

"Well"—and Ahmed seemed to anticipate this exact question coming at him—"to be perfectly honest, since I am not your primary and don't know all of your health history, my answer to that would be that the pill does work ninety-nine percent of the time if it is used *perfectly*. Since people aren't perfect, or may have some…issues, we'll say, then you have to consider the effectiveness might be closer to around ninety-three, maybe even ninety-one percent. So"—and his eyes smiled again—"certainly your pregnancy is not impossible."

Denna took this explanation in, holding on to the information, but unable yet to truly comprehend it.

He asked if there was anything else he could answer for Denna before he continued his rounds.

"The officer with me in the accident. Sarah. How is she?"

"Resting comfortably. Few minor injuries. Nothing more than that. Same as yourself. Well, except not pregnant."

Denna smiled.

"Anything I can get for you before…?"

"Uh…no. No, I don't think so. I think I'm okay."

Ahmed said he would be back in the morning to do a last check-in and hopefully begin the discharge process. He told her to take it easy, to rest and to eat. He also wished her good luck.

"Thank you."

Those words came out hollow, unbefitting the magnificence and purpose that now defined her continuance.

She sat on the end of the bed as he trudged off, wheeling his laptop along, but she didn't know how long before she was alone. She sat on the end of the bed as the program on the television above her in the corner kept reiterating the known information, the panel interrupting each other over breaking news, but she didn't listen. She sat on the end of the bed and wasn't worried about what tomorrow would look like, next week, next month, next nine months.

Everything was about the enormity of her here and now. Every breath. Every contemplation and consideration. Every choice.

As a parent.

Denna placed a hand on her stomach.

Nothing felt different now, but it was a stomach that would change and nourish and grow along with the new life inside.

The hand on her stomach was the hand that wore her wedding band.

She was at the mercy of awe still, not remiss in the fact that Teddy was gone, but still numb to her situation, not yet having that quiet time to reflect and account for and accept everything and everyone lost or to face the sadness that their child would never know him, and he would never know their child. Those feelings and those aches of helplessness, of survivor's guilt, of being a single parent, would come out later in their due time, when her mind had a chance to wrap itself around all that had happened. In her weaker moments, and in the middle of the night when doubts were at their most potent, they would etch away at her strength. Those doubts and those pangs of guilt would never win, but they would do their damage and make her second-guess. But for now, Denna was safe, she was healthy, and the hand on her stomach was there to establish the connection of a new relationship. To symbolize her protection of—and dedication to—the new life that now depended on her, and that she depended on.

Right now, she didn't question how she would do any of what lay ahead.

She just knew that she would.

TRANSCRIPT EXCERPT OF *WE THE PEOPLE* ON OCTOBER 3, 2021
Full transcript is available on axisnews.com

On this week's episode of *WE THE PEOPLE* on AXIS moderated by Margaret Rodriguez:

- Christopher Barnett, secretary of Homeland Security
- Neil deGrasse Tyson, astrophysicist, planetary scientist
- William Benke, commanding general, US Army Atlantic
- Dr. Moonary Taverni, neurologist

MARGARET RODRIGUEZ: I'm Margaret Rodriguez in New York. This week on *WE THE PEOPLE* we will show you *AXIS Evening News* correspondent Linda McClennan's exclusive interview with Homeland Security Secretary Christopher Barnett regarding what the *New York Times* is calling the "Incident at Echo Lake." Plus, astrophysicist Neil deGrasse Tyson joins us to talk about the science and what has been learned in the last four weeks regarding the mysterious anomaly responsible for nearly two dozen disappearances in the Echo Lake area of upstate New York. Also, in my interview with Commanding General William Benke, we will discuss the US Army's response to the crisis. And, finally, neurologist Dr. Moonary Taverni will be here in the studio to talk about the effects of the phenomenon associated with the anomaly.

It's all just ahead this Sunday, October 3, 2021, right here on *WE THE PEOPLE*.

[Cut to Intro]

[Cue to studio]

[Cue to MARGARET RODRIGUEZ]

Good morning, and welcome to *WE THE PEOPLE*. Four weeks ago the mysterious "Incident at Echo Lake" resulted in the disappearance of almost two dozen people at a small, wooded getaway in the town of Woodstock located in upstate New York. As reported, all eighteen residents of the lake community have vanished without a trace. There have been no signs of foul play. Most of a party of six camping at the site over the Labor Day weekend have also disappeared. Only one person from that group and a state trooper were able to escape the affected area. Since then, the area has been quarantined, investigated, and studied. Speaking with the office of Homeland Security, AXIS's own Linda McClennan sat down with Homeland Security Secretary Christopher Barnett to discuss this public safety threat. We now present to you that interview from Washington.

[Cut to interview]

LINDA MCCLENNAN: Mr. Secretary, let's begin by having you confirm what we know.

SECRETARY: Sure.

MCCLENNAN: AXIS News has learned that six individuals—Peter and Carrie Turnbull, Denna and Theodore Meers, and Ben and Kelsey Renmore—were occupying a house on Echo Lake over the Labor Day weekend a month ago. Five of the six, plus the homeowner of the residence they stayed in, a man named John Carey, along with the eighteen permanent residents of that lake community have gone missing. Can you confirm this report?

SECRETARY: Yes. Unfortunately, I can confirm.

MCCLENNAN: Mr. Secretary… What's happened to them?

SECRETARY: I think the best way to describe what we now know happened is to review the investigation that began following, as you mentioned, the escape of one person from that group of six and a state trooper who were in the affected zone. To protect privacy, I won't name names, but the two who escaped were adamant no one be allowed to enter the area. Both described to local law enforcement and first responders that they suffered from debilitating headaches, disorientation, and then, seemingly, as per the individual amongst the group of six when describing what happened to those in their party, the body would suddenly disintegrate. Disappear.

MCCLENNAN: Sounds rather extraordinary.

SECRETARY: Pretty unbelievable, right? Well, hearing a story like that, law enforcement sent in a few troopers to investigate the house and other residences while other troopers and the sheriff's office cordoned off the area and stationed a perimeter. Radio contact with those officers was lost—"

MCCLENNAN: And those officers never came back out of the affected zone.

SECRETARY: That is correct. Which is when my office was contacted.

MCCLENNAN: What were you told?

SECRETARY: Initially, the concerns given to us were of a possible chemical or biological entity or spill in the area. Not necessarily terrorist-related, but officials there were at a loss for explanations after the sheriff's office flew a surveillance drone into the area and found no bodies, but also no evidence of any foul play happening at the lake other than a few oddities. They were understandably concerned about the five thousand other residents in the nearby town and village possibly becoming exposed to whatever could have been in the air, ground, or water.

MCCLENNAN: Could you describe in further detail those oddities you just mentioned? What did the drone capture on its fly-through?

SECRETARY: They saw a few instances of what looked like settings, vehicles, or equipment abandoned in the middle of usage.

MCCLENNAN: As if whoever was operating that equipment just up and left without finishing their task or cleaning up?

SECRETARY: Yes. That is correct.

MCCLENNAN: You sent a team to the site. What did your people find?

SECRETARY: We worked in coordination with different agencies to test the area. We sampled the soil and water. We took a bunch of oxygen readings. We sampled the air to find anomalies. Nothing detectable. No dangerous chemicals, no toxins were present.

MCCLENNAN: How did you get your people in? I guess, more importantly, how did you get them out?

SECRETARY: Well, in the beginning we unfortunately suffered two casualties. We then began rigging each individual entering the affected zone for testing and investigation with a harness and line where we could allow them to enter and walk a limited distance and be pulled out when necessary, when they began to exhibit the signs of illness—the headaches and disorientation. Some were rappelled in from helicopters, and we were able to extract them quickly when necessary.

MCCLENNAN: Your team suffered two casualties? Even after the local state troopers office in Woodstock reported losses? That feels—

SECRETARY: We underestimated the ability of a person leaving the affected zone under their own power. Despite the reports we had been given by the two that managed to escape, it was all… pretty unbelievable.

MCCLENNAN: So the findings were inconclusive?

SECRETARY: Yes. And no.

MCCLENNAN: How so?

SECRETARY: Initially, our screening of the area came back with no definitive findings. Like I said, no detectable toxins, no chemicals, nothing that presented an immediate danger to the public. Nothing at all detectable. But then, toward the end of our investigation and study of the affected zone, we began to notice a waning in the anomaly.

MCCLENNAN: Can you describe that 'waning'?

SECRETARY: Where we had noticed communication and signal blackouts previously, suddenly there was service, a full and steady connection, and we were able to talk to our people inside the affected zone. Also, the onset of symptoms for those exposed—and it didn't seem to matter if they wore hazmat suits with respirators or not to become exposed—began to lengthen until symptoms never even presented or were mild and resolved on their own without casualty. After about seventy-two hours, it seemed the anomaly itself had dissipated.

MCCLENNAN: To this very day, almost four weeks since the onset of this incident, Echo Lake remains cordoned off. The area is deemed off-limits to the public, but you say the anomaly, as you call it, responsible for the disappearances of approximately two dozen individuals, seems to no longer be present. Why keep the area quarantined?

SECRETARY: Simply because we don't feel confident yet in removing the restrictions and allowing people to freely access the area. Studies are still being conducted at this time.

MCCLENNAN: Are there any theories as to why the sudden… evaporation of this anomaly?

SECRETARY: We cannot conclusively say this thing has "evaporated," as you put it, or if, like a weather front, it just simply moved on, pushed by wind currents perhaps. Being so undetectable makes it difficult, impossible even, to monitor or track.

MCCLENNAN: Mr. Secretary, is there a public safety threat? If this phenomenon has indeed moved on, what happened in Woodstock, New York, could likely happen someplace else. Somewhere more populated.

SECRETARY: We've issued no public safety alerts as of yet since nowhere else has reported similar problems associated with what took place in Woodstock back in early September. After four weeks, we are feeling a little more confident this anomaly has passed.

MCCLENNAN: I want to change to a more unusual topic on the same subject.

SECRETARY: More unusual than all of this?

MCCLENNAN: Perhaps I should say more unpleasant.

SECRETARY: Go ahead.

MCCLENNAN: Do you have any comment regarding the small vocal community of conspiracy theorists, and echoed by some of our more conservative peers in news broadcasting, who claim these disappearances are linked to a new satellite-style weapon being created and tested by our government that has the capability of vaporizing a person on the spot? Is there any truth to this, what would seem more like science fiction?

SECRETARY: Much as I would rather not provide any oxygen to conspiracy theories or unfounded claims such as these, which sound like something out of a James Bond movie or science fiction as you alluded to, I will go on the record as saying there is not one iota of truth in the speculation that this administration or this government as a whole has built, or is even thinking of building, such a ludicrous-sounding inhumane weapon. Not one iota of truth to that. Absolutely.

MCCLENNAN: Mr. Secretary, thank you for speaking with us today.

SECRETARY: Always a pleasure.

The Haven Apartment Complex
October 3
10:13 a.m.

Ellie tiptoed over the concrete walkway, creeping toward the wrought iron spindles that faced the exposed levels, inner courtyard, and in-ground pool (now closed with its interior drained, the cover littered with leaves of the autumn spectrum) of the Haven Apartment Complex. She shot a stink-eye sneer toward the unit of her neighbor, Mr. Serizawa, who was complaining—first in rough English before his native Japanese took over as he became more animated—loud enough to be heard through his open windows about the Wi-Fi in the building being out again. Ellie thought she picked up on some words she was never supposed to speak mixed in with the string of so many words she didn't understand. She then took a peek inside her own cracked-open front window and gave her mother the same curdled expression of disapproval as she lay stretched across the couch, loudly snoring away while *We the People* played on the TV. Ellie's mom had wanted to see the segment with Neil deGrasse Tyson because, as her mom put it, he was "all kinds of fine and brilliant." He also had "the voice of chocolate velvet," whatever that meant. Mom missed the segment though. Fast asleep.

"Hey, Elles Bells."

Ellie whipped around and jammed a long index finger against her lips in a shushing manner. Janelle, one of her mom's friends who lived a floor up in 5E, threw up both hands in surrender as if being held at gunpoint.

"Whoa, okay, child," said Janelle, but at a volume that was only a hair quieter. She tossed the long single braid of her hair back behind her shoulder, lowering her hands to adjust the obnoxiously bright green activewear top that held in place most of the larger woman's extras. "Dang. I was just coming by to see if your mama wanted to go get some coffee or an Auntie Anne's pretzel."

"Mom's asleep. She said her head hurt."

"Aw, that's too bad," said Janelle after clucking her tongue off the back of her teeth. "Well, when she gets up will you—"

An older woman in a white shirt with rolled sleeves and olive-tone capris, Mrs. Strudevent from down in 9C, her hair a staticky mix of gray and sickly yellow, came up the walkway toward them in a flurry. "Has anyone seen my—"

Ellie pressed the quiet finger back to her mouth and hissed, "Shhh!"

Janelle whipped her head back around, braided hair trailing like a game of tetherball. "Girl, why you shushing e'rybody?"

Taking that long finger from her pursed mouth, but retaining the scowl on her face, Ellie now directed it toward the safety railing where a single monarch butterfly perched, slowly opening and closing its wings. She whispered, "You're gonna scare it away."

"I'm sorry," said Mrs. Strudevent, lowering her voice and then addressing them both. "Have either of you seen my Beagsley?"

Ellie shook her head.

Janelle said, "Nope."

The older woman sighed, flummoxed. "He must have gotten out when Richard left the door open to get the paper. Mr. Arnold said if Beagsley craps in one of the stairways again, it'll be his last straw."

Janelle chuckled. "Yeah, your dog definitely has a weird fascination with pooping on the steps."

"I'm going to start checking the stairs. If either of you see him, will you grab him for me? I don't want Mr. Arnold catching him out without his leash."

Ellie and Janelle said they would.

"Thank you."

They watched as Mrs. Strudevent hurried off the way she came, rounding the corner along the inside square of the open building, bypassing an interior stairwell to stop and ask the tenants outside of 4F, who were enjoying a smoke, if they had seen her Beagsley.

"That woman has got the whitest problems ever," said Janelle with a frown that accentuated the one deep dimple on the right side of her face. She gave Ellie's chin a pinch. "Tell your mama I hope she better when she wakes. We'll get coffee later. I'll let you catch your butterfly."

Ellie smiled and waited until she was alone again to continue her pursuit. The monarch was still standing on the top rail, over now a few inches to the left from where it had last been, its antennae doing a dance while its wings had gone still. Ellie peeked in one more time on her sleeping mother, who hadn't moved at all, still chainsawing wood.

With slow, delicate steps, and her hand palm side up extended outward, Ellie inched closer and closer to the butterfly. The only time she'd ever been able to hold a butterfly was when she went to the New York State Fair two years ago, at age five, with her cousins. The butterfly garden there was an enclosure of wall-to-wall-to-ceiling of white mesh netting. Hundreds of butterflies of different types from all over the world clung to the nets, the lights, and to the people inside. Docile and curious, they would hang on the backs of shirts, the brims of hats, the frames of glasses. It didn't take much effort—mostly using the dab of feed on the end of a provided Q-tip—to coax the insect to her hand. Catching a butterfly in the wild, though, was something Ellie hadn't yet achieved.

Her chance at succeeding was about three feet away.

Then two feet.

The spotted and patterned wings flexed. Ellie paused. She didn't want to send it fleeing.

She took a slow breath, held it. The very end of her fingers trembled.

She whispered, "Come here."

Ellie leaned into her next step, the very ends of her fingers brushing the tissue-paper-thin bottom of the insect's wings as it released its grip on the iron rail and took flight the same moment a scream ripped across the courtyard below. The butterfly flapped its wings, traveling skyward into the overcast as a door on the third floor across the way flung open and out rushed a darker-skinned woman, barefoot in cropped jean shorts and a green top, whose face wore a fraught mask of terror.

"My father…my father's gone!"

Ellie backed away a step, straightening up as if a rod of rebar had just replaced her spine. The woman screamed and wailed, repeating herself. A mass of tenants came rushing out of their doors, some going to the woman to help, many others coming to gather at the rails around the inside of the Haven to watch and learn what happened.

"He's gone…he's not there anymore!"

The woman's panic became Ellie's.

"Mom?"

Ellie backed away, drifting, fading into the shadowed background until her back met the cold paved wall outside her apartment just below the open window where she couldn't recede any farther.

From somewhere else—was it out on the street? Ellie wondered—came a shout and a plea for help.

Louder: "Mom?"

Ellie turned to the open window. "Mom."

The couch was empty.

"Mom!"

Ellie shoved open the door to her apartment, went through the living room and kitchen, both bedrooms, and the bathroom calling for her mother. Ellie couldn't find her anywhere. "Mom!"

The screams continued outside.

They became numerous. Concentrated and amplified up through the courtyard by the enclosure of the perimeter's concrete walls.

Clamping both hands over her ears, Ellie cried for her mother as she went back out onto the walkway where, at least, she wasn't alone. Janelle came running back. Another commotion from the floor above had many of the tenants looking up and pointing, some went racing to the stairs, while a group attended to the screaming woman on the floor below who had since fainted. The scene at the complex, tranquil just minutes before, broke into chaos.

Confusion and terror claimed everyone's faces as the walkways and courtyards filled with frantic people. Hysteria in the form of screams and cries and pleas for help filled the air, rising out of the Haven, temporarily drowned out by the passing of a low-flying helicopter that had, branded on its side, the shield for the Philadelphia Police Department.

ACKNOWLEDGMENTS

My wife, Rebecca, always gets my dedication. If not for her, I don't know that I would have hunkered down over a decade ago and made the serious effort chasing this dream of mine to be a published author. She convinced me I could do it. For all of this, and for her, I say thank you, Becca. I love you lots.

My two kids will be excited to see their names in a book. To Maddie and Jack, thank you for being that constant source of joy and respite (and snuggles!) when I need it. I do apologize that you can't read this one just yet, but maybe in a few years.

Vern and Joni Firestone of BHC Press have opened their doors to me and have given me (and you) some incredibly beautiful editions of my books. Sometimes I take a copy off my shelf and just stare at the cover, inside cover, back cover, and flip through pages. Their thoughtfulness and care—and knowing they want to present the best possible version of my stories—inspires me to up my game. I thank them for all they've done for me, including welcoming me in and inviting me back.

From first draft to published edition, books go through many stages of edits. Thank you to the incredible editing team at BHC Press for their invaluable input. Many thanks to Joni Firestone, Alexa Nichols, Morgan Potoski, and Stephanie Bennett. I am eternally grateful for their editorial expertise.

It is never lost on me that readers make the choice to spend not only their hard-earned money but also their precious reading time when checking out my books. I cannot stress enough how much I appreciate my readers (yes, that includes *you*, the person reading these acknowledgments right now). If this novel is your introduction to my writing—welcome. If you've read others—welcome back. I hope you enjoyed this one enough to spread the word. I also hope that you stick around for what's coming next.

ABOUT THE AUTHOR

Joseph Falank enjoys writing that evokes emotion across many genres. He is the author of *Renewal*, *The Painted Lady*, *An Unexpected Visit*, and *Disconnected*. His work has appeared in *RiverLit* magazine, and he has also authored the young adult novel *Seeing*.

He lives with his wife and two children in upstate New York, where he is currently working on his next book—a novel for his daughter.

Milton Keynes UK
Ingram Content Group UK Ltd.
UKHW041708151024
2178UKWH00009B/11/J

9 781643 974095